FINDING TOM CRUISE AND OTHER STORIES

FINDING
TOM CRUISE
and Other Stories

ANNE CHAMBERS

LINDEN
Publishing Services

First published in 2006 by

LINDEN PUBLISHING SERVICES • DUBLIN • IRELAND

ISBN: 1905487 06 1

Typeset in Dante
Designed by SUSAN WAINE

Printed in Ireland by COLOURBOOKS LIMITED, DUBLIN

Contents

Dedicated to the memory of my uncle Tom Cruise

Loss of Faith

I REMEMBER the first time I saw them: Mr Farley with the sleeves of a pristine shirt rolled up to his elbows, lifting a wicker chair down from the removal lorry; Mrs Farley in a wide-brimmed hat and cotton summer dress, framed in the doorway. She saw me on the path where I had stopped on my way home from school, curious at the activity around the normally deserted Manse. She gave a cheery wave. Hesitantly I waved back and ran off across the Mall to tell my mother the news.

'Someone has come to live in the Manse.'

'And about time too. That lovely house has been vacant far too long.'

The Reverend Walter and Mrs Farley and their black-and-white terrier, Trixy, with his sharp bark and even sharper teeth, entered the lives of us children who lived around the Mall in the spring of 1964. For the five years that they lived in the Manse they brought a dimension that was new and challenging to our young and still open minds.

They came to our west of Ireland town to minister to the small Methodist congregation who lived mainly in the surrounding rural area. Reverend Farley was from County Cavan but his accent had long lost, if it had ever possessed, the flat, drawling tones of that particular part of the country but was moulded by education and travel. He was a Greek scholar with a love for and great knowledge of Shakespeare. He had a fine singing voice and played the organ in his church. Tall and handsome, in his late fifties, his classic features were reminiscent of a god or hero-like image chiselled on some ancient monument in Homeric Greece. Unlike the black-suited (and skirted) Roman Catholic clergy we were more familiar with, Mr Farley wore his round collar above a light-grey suit with a deeper grey-coloured satin inset. With his shock of black hair, speckled with grey, and his lightly tanned skin, to our childish eyes he cut a very attractive figure – for a clergyman.

Mrs Farley was small and plump, her hair drawn back from her round face in a bun. Behind her glasses her bright eyes seemed at once both jolly and shrewd. She was from Belfast and still retained the lilting cadences of one of the more pleasant-sounding accents of that city. Her ample figure was habitually dressed in a floral shirt-waisted dress. A well-worn straw hat, perched at a rakish slant, seemed an ever-constant accessory.

Even then to our young eyes, when everyone aged over twenty seemed ancient, it was obvious that she was Mr Farley's senior by a few years. They had no children and they seemed to love each other all the more because of it. You could see it in his eyes when he looked at her, and she was almost motherly in her affection and concern for his welfare. Whatever love they had left over, they gave to us children who lived nearby.

The Manse was set in the town Mall, an expansive swathe of green grass, intersected by paths and encircled by stone pillars, connected with ornate iron chains. The Mall was the focal point of all the outdoor activities of the children lucky enough to live around it. On its broad acres we played and quarrelled. In spring the chains became our swings. In summer, when cut, its grass brought the evocative smell of the country to the town and provided us with tons of hay with which to make our make-believe igloos. In autumn we ruthlessly knocked the chestnuts from the branches of the great trees that bounded its perimeter and made their russet treasures into conkers. When the snow fell we turned the straight, long path that dissected it into a exhilarating, if deadly, icy slide.

Set in a corner of our playground stood the Manse, a compact two-storey Georgian house, with an enclosed yard, to which Trixy was habitually banished when, on our arrival, he became a little too excited and playful with his teeth. The house had small railed-off gardens to the front and rear. The Methodist church was attached to the house and faced the entrance to our school, the Convent of Mercy, across the square. While the Manse and its church had always been part of our childhood geography, passing it as we did twice daily on our way to school, we knew little of what went on inside. The church of another denomination was forbidden territory in 1960s Ireland.

'John Wesley preached here in 1885, you know,' Mr Farley later told us.

We did not know who John Wesley was. Such historical figures and milestones did not feature in the selected history of our school curriculum, where the pope and Patrick Pearse tended to dominate.

The Mall had been the cricket pitch of the Bingham family, earls of Lucan, who had once effectively owned the town. Their mansion, The Lawn, the Irish residence of generations of Lucan earls, was by then the boarding school of the Mercy Convent. It was to the corner of the Mall nearest to the Manse that those of us who lived nearby rushed over from the Convent each evening after school, to play marbles in spring, skipping in autumn and our own brand of cricket in the long summer evenings.

The tradition of cricket had survived a bitter historical legacy and the departure of the Lucan family, under whose patronage it had flourished in the heyday of Empire. But the cricket played by us children in the 1960s had evolved, out of both habit and necessity, into something that would have brought a look of incredulity to the faces of its exponents in the past (as much as it did one summer to our uncle from Yorkshire!). Our brand of cricket was played with a single

9

crease and wicket, whose stumps and bails were made from anything available – long twigs or bamboo canes borrowed from somebody's garden – a bat roughly fashioned from a rectangular piece of wood and a worse-for-wear tennis ball. Willow bats, leather cricket balls and streamlined stumps and bails were not readily available, nor affordable, then in the west of Ireland. Cricket whites, protective pads and gloves did not feature in our consideration. You just took the knocks and the hits as they came.

It was through gardening, however, that we cricketers, skipping enthusiasts and marble-playing exponents alike were drawn into Mr and Mrs Farley's orbit. Our playground for all three pastimes ran alongside the front door of the Manse. If our boisterous and, at times, ill-tempered games ever disturbed the tranquillity of the minister and his wife, they never complained. Having no children of their own, they were more tolerant of our shouts and rowdy play than our parents.

I cannot recall my first formal introduction to them. For some strange reason or quirk of imagination, in retrospect, they always seemed to have been familiar at that time in my childhood. My first memory was of my friends and I sowing flower seeds in our individual plots, which Mrs Farley had allotted to each of us in her front garden.

'God loves a gardener,' she told us with conviction, and we believed her.

Their back garden was similarly divided for the boys of the locality in which to grow vegetables.

Every evening after school I raced over to the Manse to see if anything had sprouted above ground. With care and enthusiasm, remarkably absent in the way I tended our own garden at home, I troweled and weeded my designated plot. Eventually the tiny shoots emerged. Mrs Farley praised God and Mother Earth in equal measure and we became infected with her sense of wonderment and love of nature. When the flowers eventually blossomed, we bore them home like tro-

phies. Boys, more apt at pulling hair and indulging in boisterous horseplay, bore the less fragrant fruits of their labours
from the vegetable garden home to disbelieving parents.

By the time winter drew in, Mr and Mrs Farley had
become an integral part of our daily lives, every bit as much as
our parents, teachers or friends. While our garden plots hiber-
nated over the winter, we dashed with the same enthusiasm
over to the Manse after school, knocking expectantly on the
door in the surety of being ushered inside as welcome guests.
The sitting-room was small and crammed with dark furniture,
the individual details of which were of little interest to our
childish eyes. For me the sitting-room in the Manse will always
be associated with the smell of home-baking and of paraffin
oil, from the heater that glowed brightly in the fireplace. The
latter smell, normally unpleasant, evokes some of the happiest
of my childhood memories.

My childhood was lived in a time when the dictum that
children were to be seen and not heard (at least not too often)
still applied. Adults were adults and children were just that.
They were expected to know their place, not to intrude in
adult conversation, to speak mainly when spoken to. Any
transgression, any complaint by an adult about our conduct,
was regarded and dealt with severely – in our case, loss of
freedom or pocket money or extra piano practice being the
resultant penalty. To have two representatives of this remote
and all-powerful adult regime interested in us, in our work and
play, in what we said, in what we learned and what we liked,
was to us an indulgence as much as it was a rarity.

Mr Farley owned the first tape recorder I ever saw. In comparison to today's svelte machines, it was a large, cumbersome
apparatus with twin tapes and lots of buttons and dials. After
school, when we were seated on cushions around the paraffin
heater, when Mrs Farley's gingerbread men with currant eyes,
which awaited us most evenings, had been nibbled, when the
daily news of what had happened at school, what we had

learned, what we had to do for homework, had been exchanged and commented upon, Mr Farley reached for the tape recorder.

Then the butterflies began to flutter. Your mind struggled to remember the words of the song, the poem, the joke or the prayer that you were going to sing or recite into the machine. Each contributor was praised and encouraged by our adult audience. If anyone got stuck through stage fright or embarrassment, the minister and his wife gently coaxed them along. Each one of us was taped in turn. Then, to much laughter and not a little awe at how strange our voices sounded, Mr Farley played back our efforts. The inevitable knock-knock jokes, a very rapid rendition of 'The Runaway Train' (in which the singer, a boy, well-reared, out of deference to our clerical host, politely substituted the word 'hell' with a cough), a poem in Irish, a prayer, a hymn, our hosts recorded all our childish efforts with enthusiasm and attention.

My own contribution to one such recording session was the salutary tale of 'The Greedy Mouse'.

> A mouse found a piece of the richest plum cake.
> 'What a treasure,' said he, 'what a feast it will make.
> 'But what is that noise? 'Tis my brothers at play,
> 'I will hide with the cake lest they wander this way.'
> So he gobbled it all and it's easy to guess
> He became so unwell that he groaned with distress.
> The mouse-doctor came. 'Aha,' said he, 'tis too late,
> 'You will die before long, so prepare for your fate.'
> Now here's a lesson for all children to take,
> Don't be greedy or selfish, like the mouse with the cake.

Of special interest to our hosts were the prayers, especially the hymns, we performed. The 'Hail Mary' they did not seem familiar with, but the 'Our Father' we all said together, even though Mr and Mrs Farley had some extra words at the end that we had not heard before: 'For thine is the kingdom, the power and the glory.'

Our hymns, such as 'Sweet Heart of Jesus' and 'Tantum Ergo' to the more nationalistic 'Faith of Our Fathers' and 'Hail Glorious St Patrick', seemed doleful in comparison to the up-beat tempo of their 'Rolling Over' and 'Jesus Died for all the Children', which we all sang with gusto, clapping our hands to the beat. The words of the last hymn did more to explain to us the reason why we put our weekly penny offering into the 'Black Baby Box' at our convent school.

Jesus died for all the children,
All the children of the world.
Red and yellow, black and white,
All are precious in his sight.
Jesus died for all the children of the world.

Mr and Mrs Farley lived a frugal lifestyle, even by the standards of the time. Mrs Farley's clothes were neat but well worn and somewhat old fashioned. As we grew more familiar with the layout of the Manse, we often watched her prepare lunch for her husband in the small kitchen and marvelled at her ingenu-ity in making the most appetising-looking pies with leftover meat from the previous day's meal. They had come from a parish in the North of Ireland where their parishioners were more numerous and wealthy. The Methodist community in the rural hinterland of our town, on the other hand, were few and, like their Catholic rural counterparts, were mainly sub-sistence farmers with little to spare.

To supplement their modest means, Mrs Farley made plas-ter-cast figures of rabbits, cats and dogs, which she painted in bright colours and sold in local shops and at sales-of-work. We often helped her mix the plaster-cast filling in a large bowl, much the same as we did with our mothers' brown bread, fruit cake or fairy cakes. We watched in fascination while she filled the moulds, leaving them to set overnight. A few days later she hand-painted them in bright colours from little bottles of paint that she kept in a wooden box.

One particular Easter Mrs Farley made a special range of bunnies, each with a basket attached, in which she placed a small Easter egg. As I helped to carefully arrange each completed mould on a shelf out of harm's way, I fell headlong for this particular model and was determined to have one for Easter.

'How much will this one be, Mrs Farley?'

'One and nine-pence, dear.'

For someone who received three-pence for sweets, to which I was hopelessly addicted, each Sunday, one and nine-pence might as well have been a hundred pounds. But I had an uncle who was as addicted to Walnut Plug tobacco as I was to sweets and who always parted with 'a cat', as he inexplicably called the three-penny bit, when I volunteered to go to the shop for him. And who knows what relation might come to visit in the meantime?

After exhausting my uncle's patience with three trips in quick succession to the shop for his tobacco and saving, at great personal deprivation, one penny from my weekly allowance over a two-week period, I was still short ten-pence and Easter was close at hand. The money I had painstakingly gathered I handed for safe-keeping to Mrs Farley, who kept it in a glass jar on the shelf beside the rabbit moulds, which I noticed, with some trepidation, were fast disappearing as Easter approached.

Each time she added another coin to my pile, Mrs Farley would shake the jar and say with a smile, 'We're nearly there.'

The sale of a half-dozen much-coveted stamps from my collection to a horrible boy who had money to burn from a recent birthday raised another four pence. But by Easter Saturday I was still short five pence and had no earthly possibility of obtaining it in time. I had to admit defeat and tell Mrs Farley so that she could sell my rabbit to someone else.

With a heavy heart, I knocked on the door of the Manse. A smiling Mrs Farley appeared.

'I have it here for you, dear,' she said before I could tell her my embarrassed excuse.

I shook my head and tried to keep back the tears. 'I don't have the rest of the money.'

The jolly, shrewd eyes looked at me. 'Money isn't everything, my dear; it's the effort that counts. Here you are. You have earned it.'

I blurted out my thanks and ran home clutching my prize.

At a time when the notion of ecumenism had not been aired, our comings and goings to the Manse had been observed. Ireland was still bottled up and inward looking. Everyone was expected to keep to their own patch and to their own station in life. Small-town life could be small-minded and claustrophobic.

My mother was confronted by a neighbour asking if she realised that her children were spending an inordinate amount of time in the company of the Methodist minister and his wife.

'Yes, I do. And they have my full permission.'

My mother's reply left our neighbour with little opportunity for retort.

Our parents normally maintained a tight rein on our comings and goings, but they too had been drawn into the net of friendship and sharing with this special couple. The tape recorder had made its way over to our house.

It was perhaps towards my mother that Mr and Mrs Farley most gravitated. Her love of Shakespeare and her ability to quote soliloquy and speech from *Hamlet* and *The Merchant of Venice*, to her many word-perfect recitations of popular monologues, such as *The Green Eye of the Little Yellow God* and *The Gambler*, had struck a chord.

The quality of mercy is not strain'd;
It droppeth, as the gentle rain from heaven,

Upon the place beneath: It is twice bless'd;
It blesseth him that gives, and him that takes.

The amber-coloured tapes on Mr Farley's machine spun slowly around as they recorded my mother's remarkable retention and word-perfect delivery on their monthly visits to our house.

My father, who had a good singing voice, was less often persuaded to sing *Tit Willow* or *Kitty of Coleraine* into the recorder. His interest in the proceedings was likely to wane after nine o'clock, when his nightly excursion to 'the Academy', as he referred to his local, necessitated his departure. For the sake of the sensibilities of his clerical guest, who he rightly concluded would not be *au fait* with such an onerous nightly obligation, his departure duly became 'having to go to a meeting'.

Mr and Mrs Farley's monthly visits to our house, enhanced by my mother's home-made fruit cake and tea served in her best china, seemed much appreciated. Their congregation was mainly rural based and outside the duties of ministry, Sunday Service and an occasional special church event, they had little contact or much in common with them. They were interested and interesting, an ideal basis for a friendship and a guarantee of an entertaining and satisfying evening for them and for our parents where both parties learned something from the other.

My parents were not overly religious. They fulfilled their Church duties and saw that we did the same. Beyond that they were not involved with church organisations and politely declined visits from local clergy or their lay counterparts to our home, a custom then much in vogue. They preferred to keep Church interference in their family life at a respectful distance. Over time they found in Mr and Mrs Farley what we children, with our more heightened instincts had already detected for ourselves, goodness and kindness, two essential but often underrated qualities and the foundation for lasting friendship.

The Harvest Festival was a special event in the Methodist calendar, a service of thanksgiving to God for the earth's bounty and goodness. The small church was to be decked out with the fruits of a successful harvest: flowers, vegetables and crops. We thought it sounded so exciting. We had nothing like it in our Catholic calendar. Seldom was nature mentioned, let alone venerated, in our church.

Mr Farley, however, was faced with a dilemma, which he confided to my mother.

'As you know, my parishioners are not, well, spring chickens, if I can put it like that, and to decorate the church requires not just willing hands but able bodies. Mrs Farley has been somewhat under the weather recently and my creative talents, I'm afraid, leave a lot to be desired. I wonder if you could see your way to allowing the girls to help out.'

'Well, if it's not against your rules, it is certainly not against mine. They will be more than delighted to help. I'll send them over after school.'

With much excitement and not a little secrecy (to enter the church of another religion was deemed, if not by dogma then by tradition, a mortal sin) we presented ourselves at the Manse.

'Through here, girls.'

In trepidation we followed Mr Farley through a connecting corridor from the sitting-room that led into the church.

We had never been inside the church of another religion before and so we curiously inspected the interior. It seemed modest and unassuming in comparison to the ornate marble and stained glass of our parish church: simple pews, an organ loft and a raised dais with an arched entrance surrounded by a low railing on which stood a plain, wooden pulpit were the sole embellishments. And yet its very plainness evoked for me, even as a child, a sense of quiet reverence.

'No holy pictures or statues. Who do they pray to?' my older sister whispered.

At the back of the church, inside the door, an assortment of vegetables, flowers and sheaves of oats lay neatly stacked, offerings of the best of their harvest from Mr Farley's parishioners.

'Well, there you are,' he said. 'Decorate as you please. I'm sure you'll do a splendid job.'

We looked at each other in amazement as Mr Farley disappeared above into the organ loft. No one had ever allowed us to do as we pleased and so we set to with enthusiasm.

At the end of each pew we tied a sheaf of oats with a piece of string. Around the pulpit and on the arch leading up to the dais we entwined the richly coloured autumnal flowers: dahlias, marigolds, chrysanthemums, hydrangeas and the last of the sweet peas. On the steps leading up to the altar, we carefully laid our offerings of turnips, Savoy cabbage, butter-head lettuce and cauliflower. We tied bunches of onions, carrots, leeks, parsnips, broad beans and beetroot from the altar railing. In the straw baskets provided we placed apples, plums, pears, blackberries, gooseberries and, of course, potatoes. All produce donated by the parishioners was the best of each variety and had been scrubbed clean enough to eat. The flowers filled the air with their sweet fragrance.

At first we spoke in hushed tones, as we had been conditioned to do in our own church. But as Mr Farley spoke to us from the organ loft in a normal voice, we soon found ourselves responding. When he started to play the hymns we had learned in the Manse, we joined in and happily sang aloud as we tied and arranged our seasonal tributes around the altar and pulpit.

That evening when we had finished, Mr Farley led his wife from the Manse, his hands playfully shielding her eyes, to inspect our work.

'Well, my word, what a picture! I have never seen a more

beautiful display. The Good Lord must be well pleased with you and with the harvest offerings.'

Delighted, we received her praise for our artistic display and his thanks for helping out. Later, after a special treat of lemonade and a gingerbread man, we trooped happily home across the Mall, humming the hymns we had sung in the church.

We were not invited to participate in the actual harvest service. Both our parents and the Farleys knew there was a boundary that it was not then appropriate to cross. His parishioners may not have appreciated our presence and our parents had ventured further than prevailing dictates permitted in allowing us to assist. To go any further might well topple the delicate and enjoyable balance we had all achieved.

Perhaps it was the baptism of my only brother that more than anything else cemented our friendship with the Farleys and made it last long after they had left our town.

My brother's birth in a family of three girls was a special event for my parents and our extended family and friends. Mr and Mrs Farley were particularly happy for us and, while visiting my mother in hospital, Mr Farley expressed his desire to be present at the baby's christening. My mother said she would be delighted but would have to check with the priest. The priest who was to undertake the ceremony, a friend of the family, said that he saw no problem with the presence of the Methodist minister as a guest at the ceremony. On the day of the christening, however, Mr Farley arrived in the Catholic church dressed in full canonicals and, to the surprise of the priest, participated with him in christening my brother, who was baptised John.

'After St John and John Wesley,' Mr Farley said with a twinkle in his eye.

'Well,' said my grandfather, who was also the godfather, 'if he's half as good as either man, he'll do just fine.'

Our town being a small place then, the news spread like wildfire that my brother had been baptised a Methodist!

For four years Mr and Mrs Farley became part of our lives. Their kindness, their intrinsic goodness, bordering on naivety, that childlike quality, the essence of true Christianity as defined by its founder, had been picked up by the acute and responsive antennae of us children. Holiness had been previously represented by a narrow-minded religious devotion, a better-than-thou do-gooder, or by the wealthy benefactors in the town, whose names were acclaimed from the altar for their monetary contributions to the church – as if their offerings credited them with being more acceptable to God than those who paid less. Mr and Mrs Farley fitted no such category.

They were different. They were neither bigoted nor staid. Their joy in their religion was unbounded. It was full of hope and exuberance. Their belief exuded a childlike wonder, as well as a capacity for music and song and much fun, as Mr Farley's penchant for jokes testified.

'Many a sailor has been wrecked by a permanent wave!'

'Milton wrote *Paradise Lost* when he got married and *Paradise Regained* when he became a widower!'

'A distraught widow had inscribed on her husband's tombstone, "The light of my life has gone out." But happy and remarried two years later she added, "But I've struck another match!"'

They lived within the frugal comfort that their slender means allowed. Their unobtrusive assistance to people in need in the town extended across the religious divide. Many of the Catholic community had reason to thank them for their generosity, a fact that came to light only after their departure from the town. For them, there were no sterile boundaries of sect or creed, poor or rich, between man and God. God was for everyone and no one person or religion had a monopoly. They were the first ecumenists that we encountered but neither they nor us children knew anything about that and cared less. We liked them; they liked us. They were our friends.

At school the catechism was still the Koran for Catholics

in the pre-Vatican II era. The questions were direct and the answers, which we had to learn by heart, were unequivocal.

Q. Which is the one true Church …

A. The Catholic Church is the one true Church …

It was Monday, 2.30 p.m. The religion class, before we scampered over to the Manse, had begun. I was about nine years old at the time and I can still recall the day clearly and the question I was asked by the nun.

'Must everyone belong to the Catholic Church?'

'Everyone must belong to the Catholic Church and no one can be saved who remains outside it,' I dutifully replied.

I sat down after giving my answer, but something that was both instinctive and disturbing propelled me to my feet again to raise my hand and ask the nun, 'But, Sister, what about Mr and Mrs Farley?'

They were not Catholics and I simply could not imagine heaven without them. The alternative for such kind and good friends was too terrible to contemplate.

The look of astonishment on the nun's face had less to do with my temerity than with her inability to articulate an adequate response. The discrepancy was covered over by a reprimand.

'You are a cheeky, forward girl to question the teachings of the Church!'

Psychologists maintain that childhood shapes the adult, but for me personal experience is the touchstone that matters. Life is based on experience. That day at school, the exclusion of my friends Mr and Mrs Farley from a Catholic heaven was perhaps the springboard for my later loss of faith in the religion of my birth and my embarkation on a spiritual trail that someday, I hope, will lead somewhere, perhaps to a heaven where all are welcome.

Mr and Mrs Farley were eventually moved to some parish in the North. They were given little notice of their transfer, which occurred when we were on our summer holidays at the seaside. On our return we had hot-footed it over to the Manse only to find it forlorn and deserted. There was no answer to our repeated knocks: no excited barking from Trixy; no warm welcome and bright smile to usher us inside. Weeds had begun to take over the flowerbeds and the blinds were drawn in the sitting-room. My father later found out in the paper-shop opposite the Manse that our friends had indeed gone.

Perhaps it was as well that we children were not there to see them go. Friendships were important in our young lives and in Mr and Mrs Farley we had found a friendship that was special. My mother was particularly sorry not to have been there to wish them well. She need not have worried. They had not forgotten us.

A few weeks after their departure, the first letter arrived in what was to become a twenty-year correspondence between my mother and our departed friends. Every month they exchanged letters, my mother replying to their queries about the welfare of various acquaintances they had known in the town, as well as to their questions about us children, how we were doing at school, our exam results, our holidays, our friends. Later when we grew up and went away from home, through my mother's letters, they kept in touch with our progress in the wider world. In return their letters kept my mother informed about their whereabouts, their work and later about their retirement in Belfast. Their letters read as if they were speaking directly to us: full of innocent news, riddles, jokes and prayers.

When Mrs Farley died the correspondence continued unabated. It was as if Mr Farley derived consolation for his loss by writing to someone who had known them as the close and loving couple they had been. He must have missed her greatly, but his letters never dwelt in a self-pitying way on his loss, but in a joyous remembrance of his beloved wife, shared with someone who had known her: of the good times they had experienced together and the many blessings the Good Lord had seen fit to bestow on them. His undoubted belief that one day he would be reunited with her in the next world brought a vague hope and consolation to our own more faltering conviction in an afterlife.

When Mr Farley eventually entered a home for retired clergymen in Belfast, the letters continued, this time punctuated with even more jokes and short prayers. He seemed to relish news of our comings and goings now as adults, of jobs, holidays, boyfriends, our interests and hobbies, as much as he had when we were children.

The death of my father brought a flood of memories: of the impromptu sing-songs in our kitchen; my mother's home baking; her tea served in her special bone-china teacups, with their distinctive Celtic design; the glowing fire in the old range. All the minutiae of our ordinary family life had been hoarded in the mind of this clergyman, as if they were as important as his work or his scholarly attributes.

Many years later my mother decided to visit Mr Farley in Belfast and persuaded my sisters and myself to accompany her. We took a taxi from the train-station to the address on his letter. Up a short drive, past manicured, straight-edged lawns with flowering shrubs, to a two-storey, red-bricked house with its name, West Bank, written above the doorway.

Mr Farley was waiting for us. His grey eyes crinkled in a smile of welcome. He was now an old man, white-haired, slightly stooped. Despite his age, however, he still retained that attractiveness that emanated from the man within, as much as from his physical appearance. He greeted my mother warmly and playfully pretended not to recognise the 'young ladies' with her, insisting on remembering me only as 'The Greedy Mouse' of my tape-recording days. He ushered us inside to a large, dimly lit sitting-room, where a tray of afternoon tea and scones awaited us. The few hours we spent with him flew by in remembrances and anecdotes and ended with a promise from my mother to continue writing to him.

'Your letters are the only ones I ever get now. They do make a difference, you know,' he said as he took her hand.

She was as good as her word and their correspondence continued for some years after our visit.

His last letter to my mother took him two whole days to compile. It was as if he derived such pleasure from writing it, from being in contact with her, that he was loath to finish it.

'Have I not done well?' he wrote at the end of the page. 'It is now ten o'clock. Bed time. I feel much better that I have written this letter to you …

'Morning has come. It is just 7.15 a.m., quite early. I do not lie on in bed, just thinking. It could be good. It could be bad. God bless all of you. You mean so very much to me.'

Then the letters from him suddenly stopped.

'I wonder if Mr Farley is ill. It's not like him not to have written,' my mother said while I was home on a visit from Dublin.

She wrote to the matron of the retirement home asking about him. The reply informed her that the Reverend Walter Farley had passed away the previous month. It was a peaceful death, the matron said.

And it was no more than our old friend deserved.

The Vote

I N H E R D E S I G N A T E D C H A I R to the side of the fire, she sat alone, her grey head slightly tilted as she stared into the mock coals of the electric fire. The only sign of movement came from her wrinkled hands as they toyed with a lace-edged, crumpled handkerchief on her lap. The coal-effect reflections drew her gaze and her faded blue eyes stared hypnotically at the make-believe flames.

She thought longingly of the fire in her own home. Her cottage near the crossroads, with its small garden to the front, which she had tended with enthusiasm and care since the first day she had come to live there as a young bride. She thought too of her snug kitchen, the cockpit of her world, where she had spent the greater part of her life, caring, cooking and cleaning, first for her husband and then for her son. She could picture the open fire, the dresser with its array of delph and pottery. She could smell the bread baking in the oven. Around that open hearth she had chatted to her neighbours when they came to visit. Later, in the small hours of the night, she had sat before the dying fire, content in her own company.

A real fire, she recalled, of cream-coloured wood and black turf, which she stacked and stoked with the dexterity born from decades of experience. She remembered the acrid smell of the burning fuel and especially the vibrant flames, constantly changing shape and colour. The fire then had been her companion and her comforter, another live being. It stayed with her into the small hours of the night, and even into the new day, when in the morning she blew the still-warm coals into life again, the first task of each new day.

But her son had decreed that her open hearth was danger-ous, a fire hazard, he said. It was one of the reasons, the only reason she had come to realise, he and his wife had insisted that she move in with them.

'She'll burn the house down and herself with it, and we'll be blamed for letting her live on her own, for not taking her in,' she had overheard her son say, as he argued with his wife, who had not seemed happy about the prospect of her coming to live with them.

'There's a brand new nursing home after opening the far side of the town. All mod cons. Maybe she'd be better off there. With people her own age.'

'We'll try her here first. See how it works out.'

'Well, don't expect me to wait on her hand and foot. She's your mother. I've enough to do with you and the kids as it is.'

The old lady had not wanted to leave her own house. She was still capable of looking after herself and, realising her daughter-in-law's reluctance, more anxious still to remain where she was.

But her son was adamant. 'I won't have people saying I left my mother to fend for herself. How could I live it down?'

His words were those of obligation and duty, not of love. If their positions had been reversed, if he had had to depend on her, she knew that her love for him, her flesh and blood, would have been her only motivation.

After two years she still missed her fire sorely. When she had lived on her own, in her own house, the fire had been her entertainment, better than any television. How often of a still evening or a stormy night her imagination had been fired by the shapes, colours and effects in the flames and coals. As she stared into their glowing depths, she had seen red sunsets and golden dawns, castles, cities, strange and exotic creatures. Occasionally, when the blue flame flared among the coals, it correctly pre-dicted imminent rain and forewarned her to postpone her shop-ping trip to town for another day. The predictable unchanging shapes in the coal-effect equivalent in her son's house gave no such entertainment or predictions. Yet, she supposed, it was safer than the real thing and her daughter-in-law was saved the trouble of cleaning out the ashes every morning.

It was strange, she thought, that despite living in the company of others, she felt lonelier than she had ever been. When she had lived on her own, she had never felt that way. Within the four walls of her cottage, surrounded by her personal treasury, her furniture, household objects, the personal effects accumulated over her lifetime, she felt cosseted and entertained with the memories they evoked, which, in turn, banished the loneliness. Now, despite being in the company of her son and his family, staring into the coals was her only pastime.

In her own home she had had freedom to do much as she liked. If she wanted a lie-in in bed in the morning she could. The fact that she never did did not matter. She knew she had the choice. If she wanted to go shopping she could choose the time and the day. Now she was at someone else's beck and call: when she must rise and go to bed, when she must eat, whom she could see. She seldom, if ever, went to town now. Her friends, the few still alive, had stopped calling to see her after she had moved in with her son. The welcome, warmth, conversation and hospitality, the freedom that she had extended to them in her own house, were distinctly absent in her new abode.

Her son had brusquely shrugged off her suggestion of inviting her long-time friend Ellie in for a chat. 'We have no time for entertaining in this house.'

She knew he was right. Nobody seemed to have any time to do anything but rush in and out of the house. Everything was always in a state of movement and panic. She recalled the quiet, leisurely days in her own kitchen, when the only sound to break the silence was the ticking of the clock over the mantelpiece. Her everyday household chores she would arrange and manage in her own time and at her own pace. Now she had nothing to do and there was nothing she could do. This was not her own domain. Another woman ruled the house and she was merely a tolerated encumbrance. And as such she knew she appeared to everyone, a useless burden, someone who needed waiting on, better off in a home; better off dead. For someone who had spent her life looking after others, as well as herself, this sense of worthlessness caused her most pain of all.

Around her in the room her three teenage grandchildren were grouped before the computer, oblivious to her presence. When not playing their computer games, or watching TV, they sat, microphones fixed to their ears, heads bobbing, for all intents and purposes like the novelty dog fixed at the back of her son's car, to the beat of the music from their CD players and iPods.

When she had lived in her own house she had been central to their lives. How they had loved to come and visit her then.

'Gran, Gran, we're here!'

With warm hugs and kisses she greeted them at the door. Happily they flew inside, knowing that for the few short hours, free from the vigilant eyes of their parents, Gran would spoil and pamper them with her home-baked cakes and scones, give them her undivided attention, listen attentively to their stories. When the fateful knock on the door announced the arrival of a parent to take them home, she would slip a 'little something' unnoticed into their pockets, to spend as they pleased the next day.

Now, unless ordered by their parents to perform some specific chore for her, they scarcely even noticed her. Their smiles were few and fleeting. They seemed too busy, too preoccupied to stop and chat. And so she had lost interest in them. They in turn had become distant from her. She no longer asked them questions or listened to their chatter. Their shouts and cries now sounded muffled to her ears, as if coming from a long distance away.

Lately, most conversations in her son's house sounded the same way, as if they were taking place at a distance. Perhaps the fact that she contributed so little to the conversation that wafted around her made her interest tend to wane. It was difficult to maintain an interest when she was seldom included in the family discourses, rarely addressed directly, her opinion never requested. When her son and his wife discussed household and family affairs, they did so in whispers or in coded language that always gave her the feeling of being an eavesdropper. But what hurt her most was that her grandchildren rarely spoke directly to her any more. Instead they addressed their remarks concerning her to their parents.

Like the day before yesterday at dinner, when they were seated around the table, her grandson had asked his father: 'Can Gran vote in the election, Dad?'

'Yes, she'll be voting. Three votes from this house for the party, guaranteed.'

'I think Jim Maguire's cool,' her granddaughter put in. 'I'd vote for him if I could.'

'His crowd,' her son said contemptuously, 'never got a vote from this house and never will.'

Their conversation receded and became distant as the old woman continued to eat her food in silence.

Why was I not asked if I was voting, she thought. I could have answered for myself. Do they not know I'm here? Do they not see me? Have I somehow become invisible?

She could never accurately put her finger on the time her family had ceased to regard her as a person with a voice and a mind of her own. Perhaps it had started when her grandchildren had begun to grow up and her usefulness to them and to their parents as a child-minder had diminished. It had hurt her most of all when the children had stopped talking directly to her because she had loved them very much. Now, however, it was difficult to feel the same way about them; they had grown distant from her and she from them.

Visitors to the house had, over time, she noticed, adopted the same attitude to her. When her son's friends or neighbours came to call, apart from the usual initial pleasantries and the inevitable 'you're a great woman for your age', she was left alone in her corner while the conversation flowed around her.

It was not that the content of their conversation was beyond her comprehension. She could ably discuss any of the topics they raised, centred as they were on the community in which she lived, the land, the weather and, most recently, the general election. But ignored, she sat quietly in her chair folding and unfolding her crumpled handkerchief and soon their voices receded in her mind.

Even when the election canvassers had called to the house, she had heard the party candidate, Tim Quigley, say to her son and daughter-in-law, 'I know we can count on three votes from this house, but will the old lady be up to getting to the polling station?'

'Oh, she wouldn't miss voting for the party for anything,' her son had replied.

Everything was decided for her as usual: whether or not she was going to vote and for whom she was to vote.

She had her own opinions on the parties and the candidates. She had often smiled to herself as she watched their antics on television over the past weeks as they issued their mandatory lists of idle promises. She had seen and heard it all before, long before the days of television, when she had endured their 'live' performances at the open-air election rallies in the village and outside the church gate on Sundays. It had hardly changed an iota since and, she reckoned, never would.

But at least voting down at the local schoolhouse on election day would be a break from her mundane and lonely existence and she was looking forward to it. She might even meet someone she knew.

On election day the trip to the local school took just a few minutes. Outside the school the canvassers of the different parties milled around and handed out their coloured propaganda to the voters. Tim Quigley was on hand to help the old lady out of the car.

'Isn't she great to make the journey?' he said to her son, as he led her towards the schoolhouse.

'Nothing would keep her away,' her son replied.

The old lady remained silent as they continued to talk over her head.

'Taking care of your own, Tim,' she heard a humorous voice say. The old woman turned around to see the handsome figure of Jim Maguire coming towards them.

Ignoring her son, the young candidate for the other party shook the old lady by the hand and addressed her directly.

'Hello, Mrs Martin, I'm so glad to see you out and about again.'

'Well, it is nice to be out and about,' she replied.

'I miss seeing the light in your house, you know, since you moved. I always looked out for it on my way home from meetings. It was like a beacon. Made me feel that I wasn't the only one left in the world when I passed by late at night.'

She smiled. 'That's nice to know.'

'Well, you take good care of yourself.'

Jim Maguire strode away.

The old lady's son frowned as he looked after him.

'He's looking confident.'

'Don't know why. He won't be getting many votes in this area, and that's for sure,' Tim Quigley said with certainty. 'We'd better get her inside,' he said as he led the old lady towards the door of the schoolhouse.

Inside the polling centre, the old lady collected her voting paper. A smile brightened her tired eyes as she made her way slowly but purposefully into the polling booth.

'Well, that's that for another five years,' her son said to his wife as they drove home after casting their votes. 'A solid three votes for the party.'

He did not see the smile that hovered on the old lady's lips as she thought to herself. Two votes, son. Jim Maguire's got one vote that he didn't expect.

The Hatbox

THE POSTMAN'S rat-tat-tat on the door announced the arrival of the hatbox.

'I'll get it – I'll get it. It's my turn.'

The arrival of the hatbox from Dublin was a biannual event in our childhood calendar. It occurred in early spring and autumn and we seemed to instinctively know the exact date of its delivery. The urgency of the postman's knock – who, not being accustomed to balancing such an ungainly parcel on his bicycle, was more than anxious to off-load it – was an added clue. My sister and I rushed to the door, each of us determined to be the first to relieve the postman of his burden and to bear it triumphantly into the kitchen to my mother.

As long as I can recall, hats and my mother were synonymous. Headscarves seemed to be the preferred headwear for the mothers of our friends. But for our mother, who never wore a headscarf in her life, there were few occasions in her daily routine that did not warrant the wearing of a hat.

My mother was the Imelda Marcos of hats. She possessed a large and varied collection. They were stored, each wrapped carefully in tissue paper, in hatboxes of a sturdy nature that reposed out of harm's way (our way) on top of her wardrobe. Inside were hats for every conceivable occasion: from shopping to holidays, from christenings to funerals, for rain and for sunshine.

There were casual hats and formal hats and they came in an endless variety of shapes and sizes: wide-brimmed and medium-brimmed, cloche, sailor, pill-box, bowler, toque, New Yorker, boater. Some had a light net that covered the face to nose level but, by the 1960s, were beginning to be considered somewhat outmoded. Some hats were turned off the face, some dipped downwards, others sloped at an angle; some sat precariously on top of the head.

For winter there were hats of felt, velvet, corduroy and light wool; for summer, straw, sisal, cloth and canvas. There were special hats reserved for formal outings such as Sunday mass, visits, weddings, the occasional christening and the more numerous removals and funerals. The colours were as varied as the styles. But for every outfit in her wardrobe, coat, suit or dress, my mother possessed four or five hats to go with each.

My mother wore hats as anyone else might wear a coat or a cardigan. They were simply an essential part of her wardrobe. She would as soon walk barefoot as leave the house without a hat. Whether walking or travelling by car, bus or train, she had a hat to suit every journey. Even for our annual summer holiday to the seaside, she chose the hat to wear on the beach more with an eye for fashion than for the protection it afforded her from either the sun's rays or from unseasonable rain. Sunday mass was the catwalk for the newest arrivals to her collection, where they could be viewed by a captive audience as well as compete with the opposition.

She chose each hat to suit the particular occasion or situation and to complement the suit, coat or dress she wore beneath. She made her selection with care, assessing every model, fitting each on in turn, label to the back (the correct way, she told us), turning and dipping them, critically appraising the effect in the mirror until the right look was achieved.

My mother's infatuation with hats had always been part of her make-up, even as a child. She often recalled 'going to the milliner', one of which was attached to any retail outfitters worth the name in the 1920s. There her own mother would have her fitted for a new hat twice a year, summer and winter.

A round mould, like a pudding bowl, made of white meerschaum, was firstly placed on her head to gauge the required size. Then the milliner and her mother debated the design of the hat, as to shape, brim size, colour and any accessories, such as ribbons, buckles or buttons, required. Inside the space of a week the new hat was ready and the sense of excitement, which as a child the wearing of a new hat evoked, remained with my mother all her life.

In her adult life, like all tall women, my mother was said to be able to 'carry a hat' of almost any size. The wide-brimmed ones gave her an elegant look; the head-hugging ones emphasised her best features.

The build-up towards the arrival of the hatbox from Dublin began some weeks beforehand. A critical scrutiny by my mother of the year's spring or autumn range of 'just arrived' models at Menzies, Pims, Kelletts or Maceys in Dublin, as illustrated in black and white in the daily paper, was firstly undertaken. With intense concentration she perused the models displayed and read the accompanying description, which, before the advent of colour, was, of necessity, detailed:

> Wool Melusine felt hat, in cloche, high-crowned style, trimmed with wide band of Petersham ribbon with smart bow. Choice of rich burgundy or classic beige. Price 21/11.

Another described

> a perky straw, linen toque-style hat, delightfully caught with deep velvet bow, front-trimmed in white or soft grey with contrasting bow trim. Price 39/11.

Yet another, at 42/6, enthused about an Easter bonnet:

> a deep bucket-cloche in oatmeal sisal. The crown is decorated with draped silk chocolate brown ribbon, threaded through a single buckle and fanning out into a gathering of ribbon at the front. Available in lilac, beige or pink.

In her calligraphic handwriting, with fountain pen and ink, my mother then wrote her choice of hats and colours to the store, with the request that they would be posted to her on approbation for one week. Such were the times and the credit-trustworthiness (of hat-lovers at least) that no payment was requested by the hat shops in Dublin for this unique service they provided for their regular country customers. In due course, in the space of about two weeks, the hatbox arrived.

As one or other of us children bore it into the house, my mother's face lit up in anticipation of what lay inside. But that pleasure had to be postponed. The hatbox remained unopened until my father arrived for lunch, or what was then called 'dinner'.

'Leave it in the sitting-room until your daddy gets home,' my mother said as she prepared to serve dinner.

For around the hatbox was a sturdy wooden frame that protected the precious contents from the rigours of the train journey from Dublin. A hammer was required to prise the wooden structure apart in such a way that the nails would not bend, so that they could easily be tapped back into place when the box was being made ready to post back to Dublin. My father was deemed the only person suitably qualified in the house to undertake such a complicated procedure.

The opening of the hatbox showed us children a side to our parents' relationship not generally displayed. Like most parents in 1960s Ireland, affection was rarely openly demonstrated between them, and my father, in any case, was not a demonstrative man. Like most marriages, their relationship had become predictable and mundane, with little outward signs remaining of the love that had attracted them to one another initially. The opening of the hatbox seemed to revive feelings and emotions dimmed by time and familiarity.

'Get my black screwdriver and the hammer,' my father said as he sized up the bulky package that, after dinner was over, we had placed before him on the table.

I raced to the scullery where he kept his toolbox and extracted the required implements.

We watched closely as my father carefully loosened the nails with the flat head of the screwdriver and prised them carefully from the wooden protective frame with the hooked end of the hammer. Carefully he released the hatbox and handed it to my mother.

We children pressed closer as my mother lifted the lid. Inside was a deep covering of gleaming white, smooth tissue paper. Slowly my mother removed the top layers until, like eggs in a nest, the hats, lying one within the other, were exposed.

My mother took them out and examined each in turn. Then making her selection of the one she liked best, she went to the mirror and placed it on her head, turning and tipping it until she got the desired angle.

Then, her eyes bright with anticipation and happiness, she turned and asked: 'Well, what do you think?'

'It's lovely,' we children chorused.

And indeed it was, that hat above a face whose fine features were accentuated by the sheer pleasure and excitement she derived from the moment.

But my mother's question was not directed at us but to our father, who still lingered in the background, not showing any apparent interest in the proceedings but still not willing to leave. It was his approval that still mattered.

For a moment he looked at her, perhaps in the way he had looked at her when they had first met, when whatever attraction that had drawn them together had brought that self-same look to his face. A time before we children had come along, who, perhaps, in our own demanding way, had contributed to widening the gap that time, with its devastating ability to uncover the hidden faults and shortcomings in those once considered irreproachable, had riven between them.

My father's eyes crinkled into a smile as he nodded. 'That

one suits you,' was all he said but, for that moment, it was enough. Invariably that was the hat my mother chose.

But not before the other hats were all duly tried on, not once but many times over the space of the time they were entrusted to her, before she made her final choice.

A further letter regarding details of her purchase and a postal order for the correct amount were both placed in an envelope in the box on top of the hats being returned. The tissue paper was replaced and the lid secured. Then with her pen she deleted her own name and address on the outside of the box and not once, but twice, on two different sides (just to be sure), substituted the name and address of the shop in Dublin.

Then my father would perform his part of the ceremony and refit the box inside its wooden frame, finally tapping the nails with the hammer into place.

'Well, that's that,' he said, handing my mother the box and walking away.

One of us was then selected to carry the box to the post-office where it was weighed and stamped, the clerk commenting on its unusual shape.

'It's a hatbox,' my mother explained.

Looking at the hat she was then wearing, he smiled admiringly at her.

'Not every woman can wear a hat, you know,' he said as he took the hatbox and placed it before an open hatch on the counter behind him.

We watched as a pair of arms emerged from the hatch and the hatbox disappeared from view, and with it weeks of anticipation for us children and a brief rekindling of an emotional spark from another time for our parents.

Guns and Roses

'She's not your sort. You're fighting everything she and her kind stand for,' his older brother had told him. 'Nothing can come from it. Get out of it while you still can.'

The young man stubbed out the cigarette in the brass ashtray on the table between them.

'There's nothing to get out of,' he said quietly and left the room.

As he let himself out the back door of the house he shared with his father and brother, he took the evasive steps that by now had become second nature. In the deep pocket of his trench coat, he felt the cold steel of the .25 Browning automatic. Strange, he thought, how something given to him by the enemy should imbue him with such a feeling of reassurance.

For a moment that night, frost-clad, his breath and that of the captured Black and Tan officer mingling in a cloud above their heads came into his mind.

He had disarmed his prisoner of his regulation revolver and, from inside his tunic, had extracted the small handgun. He had never seen a more finely crafted weapon. Its polished walnut barrel was inlaid with mother-of-pearl. As he had balanced the revolver in his hand, the Tan had said: 'Glad there is something British you Irish appreciate.'

He had looked at his captive smiling nonchalantly in front of him. The Englishman had courage. He remembered wondering if he would have shown the same if their positions had been reversed.

'Oh, we appreciate a lot about you British, believe me,' he had replied light-heartedly. 'But not your rule.'

'I'll remember that, old chap, next time.'

The irony was not lost on either of them. Each understood the rules of the deadly game and the grim consequences of the capture.

By a hair's breath the Englishman's life had been reprieved that night on instructions from headquarters, carried by a dispatch rider who had cycled like the wind from the town. His prisoner was considered by HQ more valuable alive than dead. He recalled his own sense of relief. It was one thing to kill in the heat of battle, another to have to kill in the premeditated way of execution.

'Take him into headquarters,' he had ordered his corporal.

As he was being led away, the English officer had stopped before him, clicked his heels and saluted. He returned the salute and, on a whim, flicked open the barrel of the Browning still in his hand, emptied the cartridges and handed the gun back to the officer. The Englishman shook his head and smiled. 'You keep it. A memento of the best of British.'

And he had, the gun, in a strange way, becoming his lucky emblem through the war.

In the darkness he located the stile, fashioned from blocks of wood, at the end of their garden. He cleared the boundary stone wall into Mrs McGrath's garden next door. She was a staunch supporter who had often given misleading information about his whereabouts first to the Tans and, more lately, to the Free Staters. He did not leave through the back of her garden, in case her house was been watched, but clambered over the walls of two more adjoining gardens, before finally emerging cautiously into the narrow street.

He knew in his heart that his denial to his brother about his relationship with her was as equally suspect as his brother's accusation had been. Since meeting her, emotions and feelings hitherto stifled by convictions that had uncompromisingly propelled him into manhood before his time, had become unleashed. He had not had time to experience an adolescence, to develop his talents or his emotions, but had been hurled headlong into a guerrilla war against an empire. That had become his all-consuming passion, replacing everything else.

He had grown up in a hurry, developed into an intelligent combatant, a military strategist and weapons expert of whom any army would have been proud. He had been trained and disciplined by experts: former soldiers of the British army, the best-trained army in the world, the army that had become his bitter adversary, or the maverick part of it that had been unleashed in Ireland.

His own decision to take the oath and volunteer for active service had not been inspired by any grand patriotic notion. The violation of the sanctuary of his home by the thugs sent over from England, in a last ditch effort to stem the swelling tide of radical Irish nationalism, had ignited his conviction. The catalyst for him had been a rifle butt sweeping across the shelves of the oak dresser in the kitchen and the cups, saucers, plates and his mother's treasured collection of butter-milk jugs being dashed to the floor by an Auxiliary, from whose eyes shone a look of unhinged hatred, while his companions held him and his father against the wall, rifle barrels to their throats.

As he silently endured the racist taunts and threats hurled at them by Cockney and Geordie accents within the wrecked interior of the room that, more than any other, was sacrosanct to the trivia and normality of his family life, and which encompassed most memories he had of his dead mother, it was as if these strangers had violated his person. He knew he would never, could never, endure that again.

At twenty-four he had already become a legend. Men older than him looked up to him, wanted to shake his hand, wanted him to honour them with his company, to introduce him proudly to their wives and families as their friend, the patriot, the brave resistance fighter. The adulation had not gone to his head. He took their accolades in his long stride, with an attractive disarming modesty and not a little humour. In their company he would rather sing for them, his tenor voice extolling the virtues of the Star of the County Down, or the attributes of the Salley Gardens, than relate the awful adventures into which life for three years had led him: living on the brink, mind and body taut, straining to listen at the least sound around him, in case it was his last; the ambushes; the imprisonment and daring escapes – life on the run among the mountain ranges and windswept bog lands of north Mayo; the enemy killed; the comrades saved; the excruciating pain of enemy lead in his leg, treated with iodine in some wind-blasted refuge among the heather. At twenty-three he had read his own death notice in the *Irish Independent*. But through the pain and deprivation, the ultimate goal of freedom endowed the sacrifices he had made and the pain he endured, all of it, with a mind-numbing nobility.

And where had his great crusade for freedom brought him in the end? Down the ignoble cul-de-sac of a Cain and Abel vendetta. Former comrades to whom he would have once entrusted his life, with whom he had shared his last smoke among the wet bracken along the mountain foothills, as they lay in ambush for the Black and Tan tender, one whose life he had saved, neighbours and friends, were now as much the enemy as the Tans and Auxiliaries had been. Shaped and soldered by higher motives of freedom and nationhood, fed by the rhetoric of Tone, Pearse and the great Fenian veteran O'Donovan Rossa (in whose funeral cortège, as a boy, he had marched in the guard of honour to Glasnevin cemetery in Dublin) he found it difficult to comprehend the mindset of former friends who now looked at him with the same hatred as the Auxiliary had in his mother's kitchen.

'Bloody republicans. Hanging's too good for ye.'

War-weary and compromising, his own people, for whose

freedom he had fought and sacrificed his youth, now derided him and his companions.

Tone and Pearse had never conceived that their high-minded ideals would have descended into such an ignoble, shameful bloodbath, as Irishman fought Irishman with the same intensity with which they had once combined against the British. The Fathers of the Revolution had bequeathed soldiers-in-the-field like himself no theories or directions to validate the terrible actions he was ordered to carry out against his fellow countrymen. Civil war was an ignoble, dirty business and he despised it. But he was a soldier, a captain, a leader of his unit, and orders, no matter how loathsome, had to be obeyed. He knew no other way.

His soldiering life had ill-equipped him for relationships with woman. His was a male-oriented world, revolving around guns, military manoeuvres and tactics. His comrades were his friends, many of whom were as young and as emotionally inexperienced as himself. The older men in the unit, seasoned in the ways of the world, many ex-British Army veterans, boasted of their conquests and spoke of women in a snide, sexual way that made him feel uncomfortable. They taunted the inexperience of their younger comrades, but stopped short at him. Although older than him, they were used to having younger men in command over them. The British Army promoted by birthright and privilege more often than by ability, as the soldiers at the Somme and Ypres had found out to their cost.

No such discrimination applied in the ranks of the Irish Republican Army. He had won his stripes as a captain at twenty-two the hard way. He had obeyed his orders to the letter and had built up the trust of the men in his unit, remaining one of the boys until it came to action. Then the captain in him took over and the comradeship was replaced by leadership and an unequivocal belief in his own ability. Then his soldiers knew better than to question or cross him. It was the same when their sexual banter made him walk away from their company, as if putting a distance between him and their discussion. They sensed his discomfiture and looked in silence after his tall figure.

Apart from the Cumann na mBan women, who, for the most part, were as tough as the men in his unit, his relationships with women had been few. His mother, who had died when he was sixteen, had been the only woman he could truly say he had known, that is until he had met this girl.

As a young fellow, his mother had encouraged him to read. In the aftermath of the Easter Rising and the heightened nationalistic emotions that the subsequent executions and reprisals had awakened throughout the country, it was as if she thought that books might somehow become a shield and prevent him from being drawn into the increasingly confrontational situation. His older brother had already been lured into the ranks of the Irish Republican Brotherhood.

'For God's sake, for my sake, don't follow your brother. Stay at school and get a job. One of you is enough to have to worry about,' his mother had begged him.

She bought him books she knew would engage and occupy his young mind, in the hope that he would remain aloof. He had read everything by Sir Arthur Conan Doyle, *A Study in Scarlet* and *The Adventures of Sherlock Holmes* being particular favourites, as was Dickens' *David Copperfield*. *Tom Brown's Schooldays* he had read and re-read many times. All the books available were English-oriented and were about people and situations far removed from his own background, but he had enjoyed them nonetheless.

Strange that it should be someone like this girl, regarded by himself and everyone else as more English than Irish, who had introduced him to his own literature. Or maybe not, he thought, as he recalled her shrug and mild reproach when on their first meeting he had asked her what she was doing at a Gaelic League meeting.

'To learn about my culture,' she replied. Her accent, her clothes, her very demeanour, to his eyes, were English.

'*Your* culture?'

The words had left his mouth before he could stop himself. How could anything to do with the Gaelic League, Irish history or Irish literature be of interest to her sort or be deemed her culture?

Her accent, the Georgian manor-house outside the town where she lived, her father, a former Royal Magistrate in the British establishment, all pointed the finger to a background as English as anything he had read about in his books. She had seen the disbelief on his face and a faint smile made her lips curl enticingly.

'What is your name?'

He told her as they sat next to one another in the back row of the town hall during the intermission.

It was a lecture on the legends of Fionn MacCumhail and the Fianna, given by a professor from some university in Dublin.

He had slipped into the hall during the lecture, when all eyes were on the speaker, to avoid detection by anyone who might feel compelled to reveal his presence to the enemy. He had arranged with a friend for a quiet game of billiards in the clubroom upstairs after the lecture but had arrived before the lecture had finished. He had spent the previous two months in a training camp, deep in the Nephin mountains, drilling a batch of new recruits, and had been given a two-week furlough. In the dimly lit auditorium he had slipped into the first vacant seat at the back. During the lecture his gaze had wandered and he had recognised, with some surprise, who was seated next to him.

'Not an Irish name,' she told him. 'English, I would say at a guess. Do you know where your ancestors came from?'

He shrugged. 'I never thought about it much, to tell you the truth. My father is Irish, so was my grandfather. I'm Irish.

45

Beyond that, I couldn't tell you. But you're ... English.'

She looked at him in the half-light. She was about his own age, he reckoned, maybe a year older. Her auburn hair peeped out from beneath a hat that hugged her small head. Her features, it seemed to him, were in perfect proportion, nose to mouth, forehead to chin. Hazel eyes regarded him evenly. He felt himself blush under her gaze and hoped she did not notice.

'My ancestors came to Galway eight hundred years ago. Maybe they should have come to Mayo ...'

He laughed with her. 'You've got me there,' he said, while at the same time he felt annoyed by his show of ignorance.

He had never considered her sort Irish. The movement had always depicted the Protestant landed class as outsiders, the enemy of Irish nationalism, tools of the British Empire. And here he was being confronted by a historical fact that was at variance to his belief and to popular perception. Her family were possibly more Irish than his own. He had once heard his grandmother accuse his grandfather in an argument of being descended from a Cromwellian, and he had felt ashamed. The fact that almost three hundred years had elapsed did not ease his sense of disquiet that he could be descended from the blood of Ireland's most despised invaders, or that he was anything other than an Irishman through and through.

'I thought the professor's book fascinating. That's why I had to come, to hear him speak in person,' she said as they left the hall together after the lecture. 'Have you read it?'

He shook his head.

'Then you must.'

'I don't know much about Irish legends and that. I did read about King Arthur and the Knights of the Round Table.'

'But they are *English* legends.'

'My mother,' he looked at her sheepishly, 'insisted that I read anything that came to hand. To keep me out of trouble, she said.'

'And did it?'

He looked at her before averting his gaze.

'Not quite,' he said ruefully.

If only she knew, he thought. His part in the struggle would certainly be considered more than mere trouble to her kind. He was halfway up Main Street before he realised he had completely forgotten about the billiard game and was going in the opposite direction. He stopped.

'Where are you heading?' he asked her.

'Daly's Hotel. I am to meet my father there.' She noticed his indecision. 'Please, there is no need to walk with me. I thought you were merely going in the same direction.'

It was her turn to blush.

'I am,' he lied.

Turning up the collar of his trench coat, he pulled down his cap and fell into step beside her.

They had met again that same week at a play, The Countess Cathleen by W.B. Yeats, performed by the local drama group. She had talked to him about it as he had walked her to Daly's Hotel that first night and he had made certain that he got a ticket. He had not thought much of the play; it was not his cup of tea. But from his seat a few rows behind her, he had watched her absorption, her head slightly raised so that she could catch every movement on stage.

For himself it was enough that he could see her. He had thought of her often enough since their first meeting. She had came into his mind at the most unlikely times: in the middle of a game of billiards; as he read his newspaper; in his daily routine of cleaning his Browning with an oily rag; or at night-time, when he lay on his narrow bed, fully clothed and ready for flight.

After the performance he had waited around the corner from the hall, emerging from the shadows as she passed. She did not start, nor wonder why he should fall into step beside her. She just smiled at him as if she expected him to be there and that walking down Tucker Street together was the most natural thing in the world. They chatted about the play, about books they liked. He found her easy to talk to. Despite her accent, there were no airs or graces about her but a naturalness that attracted him, put him at his ease, made him feel as if he had known her all his life.

He realised that he felt more comfortable talking to her than he did to Mrs McGrath's two daughters next door. They always seemed to cross his path and, by the knowing glances they threw at him, always gave the impression that there was some secretive meaning in the most innocuous and briefest exchanges he engaged in with them. It was some female game they played in which he had little expertise or interest.

They left the lights of the town behind and headed into the twilight of the countryside.

'Are you not afraid, walking home alone so late?' he asked, genuinely amazed that she had no one to accompany her from town.

'What's to be afraid of? Who would want to harm me in my own country?'

He looked at her, wondering if she was being sarcastic, disingenuous. He caught her look and her eyes told him that she was not. She was merely expressing what she thought to be true.

'These are troubled times, you know, for everyone.'

Her hazel eyes, luminous in the gathering darkness, appraised him. 'Especially my sort, is that what you mean?'

He shrugged. There was no use beating around the bush, if it meant making her more aware of the danger. 'You should be a bit more careful.' He smiled at her. 'Not everyone appreciates how Irish you really are.'

'Now you are laughing at me,' she rebuked him with a smile as they stopped at the open iron gates.

He looked up the long avenue that led to her house. She followed his gaze.

'My father is the most understanding and generous man I know, both as a father and,' she looked at him, 'as a magistrate. Nobody could possibly wish him or his family any harm. He spoke out against the Black and Tans, even wrote letters to the papers. He chose not to leave like the rest after the Treaty but offered his services to the new Free State.'

He nodded. 'I know. But not everyone agrees with the Free State.'

'Do you?'

Her question was as simple as it was direct.

He looked away and contemplated the avenue once more.

'We were short-changed.'

'I thought it was freedom to attain freedom, according to Michael Collins.'

'The fight was for an all-Ireland republic. Now we are left with neither one thing nor another. Soldiers, no matter how brave, do not make politicians. Collins versus Lloyd George?' He shook his head. 'It was no contest. He should not have done a deal with the British. He should have fought on.'

'Like you?'

'It's nearly dark,' he said abruptly. 'I'll walk you up to the house.'

They walked on in silence. She knew by his demeanour that he did not mean to continue that line of conversation and the natural reserve of her upbringing prohibited her from questioning him any further. Where the avenue spread out before the gracious lines of an ivy-clad Georgian house, he stopped.

'Well, here you are,' he said somewhat lamely, conscious that he had spoiled the easy rapport that had developed between them.

'You can come in, if you like.'

She said it casually, as if he were one of her friends, and he appreciated it. There was no sense of class distinction or, now that she suspected whose side he was on, political division. She was simply taking him as she found him, for himself.

'Maybe some other time.' He hoped his refusal sounded as natural as her invitation.

'Well, see you again some time.' She held out her hand.

Somewhat taken aback, he took it, removing his cap with his other. For the first time with her, he was at a loss for words. His natural inclination was to lean towards her and kiss her, but he simply lacked the courage, or whatever it took, to make the move. He felt her hand stir in his as she attempted to extricate it.

'Sorry,' he said.

With a smile she turned and walked quickly across the drive. Soon she was lost in the darkness. He listened to her footsteps on the loose gravel. A stream of light issued out as the door opened. Only when he heard it close behind her did he retrace his steps down the long avenue.

They met a few times more before his furlough was up and he had to disappear into the hills again. He had left a note for her at Daly's Hotel. They seemed to have drifted into some sort of relationship that he could not quite fathom. All he knew was that each time he left her, he was more anxious than the last time to see her again. While she did not voice her opinion of him, or of what was emerging between them, she seemed content to be in his company. And for him, for now, that was enough.

On their last evening together, as he walked her back to the house, he told her that he would not be able to see her for a while because he had to go away. Her eyes, which had begun to invade his dreams at night, regarded him with a look that seemed to see inside him. He knew from their conversations over the past two weeks that evasiveness, lies, either white or black, were not in her nature and he instinctively realised at that moment that she knew exactly where he was going.

As his feelings for her had grown, he purposely kept the subject of the war, and his part in it, out of their talks, steering her away from even casual observations and comments on the political situation. That subject, if broached, he feared, would herald the end of their friendship; and he wanted it to last as long as he could, to spin out the fantasy and the feeling for a little longer, before reality sank in and his brother's words proved inevitably true.

Already they had been spotted stepping out together, although he had been as careful as he could to steer their meetings out of town – walks in the surrounding country lanes, high tea in a secluded corner of the dining-room in Daly's. But as his mother always said, windows had eyes, and none more so than in the narrow country roads outside the town. That was how his brother came to know about her. His subsequent denial to his brother, that his friendship with her meant nothing special to him, was as much to protect her as himself.

'Father heard that the houses of anyone serving the Free State government have been declared targets by the Irregulars.'

Her words brought him back to the reality of their situation. She had that knack of knocking him off balance with her directness.

'Where did he hear that?'

'A policeman came out last night from town to warn us to be on our guard.'

'Well, it's news to me.'

They walked up the avenue towards the house. It was so still, not a puff of wind, as if the countryside was holding its breath. The late autumn evening was ending in a glorious afterglow of crimson, as far to the west the sun sank in a ball of fire below the black line of the land.

'I wouldn't worry about it,' he tried to reassure her, without having any basis to do so. 'I don't see how the Cause can benefit from burning your house. After all, you're more Irish than myself.'

She smiled briefly but he saw a quiver, either of fear or sadness, he could not be sure, fleetingly touch her face.

'Father has been talking about leaving, you know. For Canada.'

'He cannot.'

Her look, a mixture of both surprise and gladness, made the moment that he had imagined in his mind, in a flash, come into reality. There was no time to think, no time to ponder the outcome, as he bent his head and kissed her gently. She pressed his lips with hers and then the moment was over. Abashed, they smiled shyly at one another, as if taken aback by their own audacity.

'Maybe Ireland is no longer safe … for any of us,' she said, and he knew that she meant for him as well.

They had stopped at the top of the avenue where it opened out into the wide space before the house. He looked up at the graceful Georgian lines: low-pitched roof, five windows, three on top and a longer one on either side of the door, with its intersected fanlight above, and three wide steps leading towards it, every aspect built in simple yet perfect proportion. Just like herself, he thought.

From a room to the right of the door, an oil-lamp cast a mellow glow through the rectangular panes of the window, spilling out over the grass verge. The house exuded a feeling of antiquity, of having being there for centuries, and yet to him, by reason of his beliefs and conditioning, it remained aloof from the ordinary life that went on outside its gates. No matter how much he would like to tell her otherwise he knew what people in the town – his neighbours, friends, his own brother – thought of her kind.

Whether that sense of difference, of apartness, with which the Anglo-Irish were inevitably tagged was now to be exploited in a more sinister way by his side, he would have to find out.

'Look, I'm sure no one means any harm to you or your family. I'll ask around – see if I can find out anything – and let you know.'

'I don't want to get you into any trouble. It's just a bit of a worry, not knowing. My father is more concerned for me than he is for himself.' She sighed.

'I never recall him being so, so … depressed about things.'

He took her hand in his and she did not resist.

'Look,' he said, 'I'm sure there is no need to worry. I promise I will get word to you as soon as I hear anything.'

His grip tightened as if he feared that she would disappear there and then. The thought of her leaving, that he would never see her again, he could not imagine. He wanted to tell her how she had become part of his life, of his thoughts: how he looked forward to meeting her and how often he had purposely inveigled their supposedly accidental encounters over the preceding two weeks. He did not know, as yet, where their relationship was going, if indeed it could lead anywhere. But the initial stage that they were in he found exciting and fulfilling, holding out, as he thought it did, a promise of something deeper to come.

'I would hate to see you have to go.'

That was all he could bring himself to say in case what he really wanted to say was rejected or caused her embarrassment. It was too early for him to even articulate his own feelings to himself, much less to her. He did not know if she had any feelings for him, other than that of friendship. If he said any more, he risked destroying their embryonic relationship before it could develop.

'And I would hate to think we could not see each other again.' She stood on tiptoe and brushed his cheek with her lips, before running quickly towards the house.

Her words imbued him with a warming glow as if a fire had been enkindled deep inside him. He had not imagined it after all. She had feelings for him and, braver than him, had risked saying it. He hurried down the driveway, his heart pounding.

As soon as he got back to the training camp, he asked the camp commandant about the rumour.

'It's all a bit muddled. I only know what I read. The Chief of Staff seems to think it's a good idea. But nothing official has come from the Army Council. So until I hear further, I know as little about it as you. Why do you ask?'

He shrugged nonchalantly. 'Just heard some talk around the town.'

'Well, your brother, being in intelligence, is sure to know before any of us. Why don't you ask him? I'm only one of the foot-sloggers.' His commandant sounded bitter and disillusioned.

He knew his brother would be the last person he could ask. He had steered well clear of the subject of his new friendship the few times their paths had recently crossed.

Over the next few weeks, in his hut hidden in the fastness of Nephin, he thought of the gracious house and the sense of tranquillity that it imbued, and he thought more often of her.

It would be a while before he would have another furlough and be able to see her, if at all. There was talk that he and the unit he was training might be ordered to link up with another further north. With the hand of both state and church now resolutely opposed to the Cause, recruits were beginning to dry up. There were fewer safe houses open to them. The Free Staters, who had once soldiered alongside them, knew too much about their movements: who might be friendly towards them, about their hiding places, weapon dumps, even about the routes they favoured across the mountains. There was talk now of amalgamating units from different divisional areas, even of disbanding entire columns.

His recruits were now all but trained in the basics of guerrilla tactics, could use and maintain their Enfields, Smith and Wessons, Webleys and the hot-potch of revolvers, pistols, rifles and shotguns that had been allocated to them from headquarters. That was all they had to fight with against an enemy that had been armed by the British. His charges were a mixed bunch of young jobless townies and the sons of subsistence farmers from the countryside around. He could spot the ones who merely tagged along for something other to do than stand at street corners, and the ones who were motivated by something more. By the time he had finished with them, whatever their initial motivation for joining, he would have them transformed into dedicated soldiers, eager for action.

At night, lying on his wooden makeshift bunk, he wondered if she was living still in the Big House, or if her father, as she had said, had taken her to Canada? Maybe he would never see her again. How could she get a message to him, even if she had wanted to? If she saw him now, training young fellas to kill and maim their own countrymen, would she, could she, feel anything but revulsion for him? He ached to speak to her, to feel the touch of her lips on his. Would she still want him to come with her to start the new life she had spoken about in Canada? It had sounded so compelling, so daring: a new world, a new start, for them both, somewhere they could be together without anyone questioning their background or their politics. Somewhere there was no past, only a future.

Over succeeding weeks news trickled through to the camp of the burnings of Big Houses around the country. He consoled himself in the fact that they had happened a long distance from Mayo. When a despatch rider from headquarters brought news that Moore Hall, a mere forty miles away, had been gutted, then he began to realise that her father's fears may have been well-founded. If the home of one of Ireland's premier Catholic families, the birthplace of the president of the 1798 Republic of Connaught, had been deemed a legitimate target, what chance had the house of a former royal magistrate of remaining immune?

He tried to reason the military advantage ensuing from such a tactic. As a guerrilla fighter he had been trained (and subsequently had trained his recruits) to ensure that each manoeuvre undertaken was essential tactically to the mission, that it had more than a good chance of overcoming the risk posed and that it warranted the men and weapons being expended. In the War of Independence, the military advantage of burning the houses of those of the landed gentry who had collaborated with the British, or who had allowed their houses to be used as bases by the British military against the IRA, had been clear. The advantage now, either tactical or moral, to the Cause of burning the houses of those who had remained and who were willing to be ruled from Dublin instead of London, by either Free Staters or, if his side won the war, by Republicans, seemed, to him, absurd.

From her he had learned that nationality was not all about religion, status or past allegiance. It was far more complex than that. Was her house not as much a part of the Irish landscape as the thatched cottage down the road from it? Was the real motivation for the destruction of the Big House something far less noble? Had plain envy and greed replaced patriotism? He tried to put such thoughts from his mind. It was not his job. He was a soldier, under oath, to carry out his orders.

His orders when they came were sudden and unforeseen. He was to take his unit not, as had been rumoured, further north, but back to a location near the Windy Gap, close to headquarters in the town. There he was to await further instructions.

They travelled by night, staying overnight in the hay shed of one of the few remaining safe houses outside Crossmolina. Their supporters were getting fewer by the day as the people, tired and frightened by the idea of Irishmen killing Irishmen, began to close their doors to them. The following night they bivouacked under the open sky, trying as best they could to take shelter under the gorse from the sleeting rain.

In the first pale light of the winter morning, he watched through his field glasses for the despatch rider he expected to come from the direction of Castlebar. He spotted him at a distance and monitored his progress, sweeping the bleak landscape around to ensure he was not being followed. As soon as the rider got near enough so that he could identify him, he gave a curt order to one of his recruits, who slithered down the wet hillside towards the road and stepped out in front of the rider. Through the glasses he continued to observe the transfer of the despatch pouch from the rider to his recruit. Not until the rider had disappeared back the road he had come did he lower the glasses.

At a distance from his men, he read his orders. Owing to the serious lack of manpower and equipment, he was, as he had expected, to join up with another unit near Foxford. But before that, the despatch stated, he was to carry out one final engagement. He heard his heart pound in his ears and he looked quickly towards his recruits, gathered expectantly in a bunch close by, fearing they had heard it too.

'After due notice is served on the occupants to vacate said premises,' he read, he was ordered to torch the house, her house, 'the property of a Free State collaborator'.

Slowly he reread the words, praying that he had made a mistake, that it was someone else's house, anybody's but hers. But the neatly typed orders read the same. Why him and why her home, he asked himself? Was it some form of punishment for becoming friendly with somebody whom his superiors, even his own brother, deemed to be the enemy? The order read so matter-of-factly. And perhaps it would have been, he thought, if it had concerned any other Big House in the country, the house of someone whom he did not know, of someone he did not love. He folded the sheet of paper and put it inside his tunic. He took a deep draw on his cigarette.

He looked out across the vast panorama of bog and moorland that stretched away towards the west. In his mind's eye he could visualise her house, in the pale light of the morning, all tranquil and unsuspecting of what was about to be visited upon it. How could its destruction possibly benefit the Cause? His unit was being withdrawn from the area, so there was no military or moral advantage to be gained. He had lived his life, his military life, like any soldier, obeying orders. Even when dubious tactics were employed by his superior officers, he had never questioned them but relied on his own ability to turn the situation around.

He had never compromised his loyalty to the Cause, which he placed above everything else, even above his own life. It was that unquestioning fealty that had driven him for the past three years to live his life on the brink. Had it also, he now wondered, more lately blinded him to the obvious? That the Cause was a lost one, that the people had had enough, that it was time to give peace a chance. He stubbed out his cigarette. Such thoughts were in the realm of politics and he was no bloody politician. He signalled to his corporal.

'Take the unit back to the farmhouse. I'll meet up with you there before daybreak. I have to attend to something first.'

'Will you be needing any of us?'

'No, no. Just a final meeting with Command before we move up country. I'll go on my own.' He handed the corporal his Enfield and checked inside his tunic for the familiar feel of his Browning.

His corporal, who had been with him almost from the start, hesitated.

'Are you sure, John? Why not take one or two of the young fellows with you, as backup, just in case.'

He shook his head. 'I'll be better off on my own, and quicker. See you at the farm.'

He raised his hand in salute and quickly set off down the hillside, half-walking and half-running, keeping close to whatever ground cover was in his path. He knew the vast, empty moorland that stretched before him, every sheep track, gully, stream, boreen, hill and hollow. Whenever they had done a job in the area, it was to this desolate, sparsely populated territory, which stretched back towards the slopes of the mountain, that he and the rest of his outfit had taken refuge, laid low, nursed their injuries, got re-supplied, until orders came for the next job, which he followed, as he had always done, to the letter, without compromise.

As he sloshed his way across a stream, he knew that this time his mission was different on at least two accounts. He was blatantly disobeying his orders and he had no plan of action.

It was nightfall before he reached her house. Its solid outline stood proud in the thin light. He paused in the shadows thrown by the high shrubbery. A solitary light shone from an upstairs window. Was it her window he wondered? It could as easily be her father's or a servant's. Keeping close to the shrubbery and to the hedge that surrounded it, he walked around the house. There was no other light to be seen. He had to take a chance.

He moved out to the gravelled space before the front door. Taking up a few pebbles from the path, one by one, in quick succession, he threw them towards the lighted window. The curtain was hurriedly drawn back and her face peered out into the darkness. Quickly he lit a match and he saw her raise a hand in acknowledgement.

Within minutes she was beside him. She stood waiting as if, like himself, uncertain how to express her feelings at seeing him again. He took the initiative and kissed her hurriedly. She smiled.

'Quite a strange hour to call,' she teased him and shivered in the damp air. 'Let's go inside.'

'I'm afraid there's no time. I have to get back.'

He took off his trench coat and placed it around her shoulders. Her eyes alighted briefly on his army tunic and Sam Browne belt. She looked away.

'You are quite the Scarlet Pimpernel. They seek him here – they seek him there. I wish it was not like this. That you could be here all the time.'

There was no point in pretence any longer. 'There's a war

on and I'm part of it. Perhaps when things settle down, we can be together more often.'

'Then it may be too late.'

She walked a little away from him and stopped at a sundial, surrounded by the withering branches of the decaying summer's roses. Here and there a few last blooms clung stubbornly on, emitting a soft fragrance into the damp night air. He followed her to where she stood. She looked up at him.

'Father has decided. He is leaving for Canada.'

'When?'

'Next week.'

He felt relief well inside him. He should be able to string things out until then, keep his orders under wraps. Once the house was vacant, the danger to her would be eliminated.

'And you? Are you leaving too?'

She shrugged. 'Except for the house, there is nothing to keep me here. Is there?'

She turned towards him, her eyes searching his face, demanding his response. He was trapped. If he told her how he felt about her, she would stay on in the house and be in danger. If he refused to carry out his orders, someone else would carry them out in his place. His brother's words came to him as a way out.

'I'm not your sort. It would never work out.'

Immediately he had uttered the words, he felt the shame of his duplicity and lie. They made him feel as much a traitor as if he had betrayed the Cause. And, he reckoned, in a way, by his disregard of his orders, he already had.

His words seemed to make her recoil. She looked at him with cold disdain.

'Perhaps you are right. I have obviously mistaken our friendship for something else. Please excuse me.'

She made to leave, but he stopped her.

'You made no mistake. If things were ... normal, no war, me just doing ordinary things ...'

Her eyes, in the semidarkness, shone with the conviction of her words, which tumbled out in a torrent.

'Then let both of us be ordinary. Come with me to Canada. We can start a new, ordinary life there together, free from all this awful war, this ...' she motioned towards the house, 'other life. Free to be ourselves, without any baggage, political or otherwise. There is nothing to hold us here. Please say you'll come.'

'I cannot.'

This time the words came out of him honestly and unambiguously. He did not have to think about his response. They were the ultimate proof, as much to himself as to her, of where their friendship stood in relation to his loyalty to the Cause that had taken over his life. At that moment he knew he could never abandon it before its natural culmination, be it in victory or, as it now seemed more likely, in defeat. It bound him by stronger bonds than his new-found friendship with her, possibly even more than the love that he sensed could undoubtedly grow between them, if circumstances had been different. He was still the soldier and the time had not yet come for him to slough that skin.

'Well, that is something *my sort* does understand. Duty comes first.'

While there was an edge to her words, there was sadness in her eyes. She took his coat from around her shoulders and handed it back to him.

'At least let me have something to remember you by.'

As he bent his head to kiss her, he heard a soft thud of something falling to the ground. He leaned down and retrieved the small Browning, which had fallen out of his coat pocket. For a moment he balanced it in his hand then, almost instinctively, he held it towards her.

She looked at him in disbelief and then down at the gun. Her fingers touched the inlaid barrel. 'How appropriate. Just as cold as your heart.'

She took the gun, turned from him and walked towards the house. The scent of the fading roses permeated his benumbed mind. He could not let her go like that, without something, a more appropriate token, a memento of what her friendship meant to him. He leaned over the straggly rose bushes and searched around until he found a few intact specimens. He felt the thorns pierce his fingers. He broke off a few stems and ran after her. She heard his footsteps and turned expectantly around.

'I will never forget you,' he said as he handed her the makeshift posy.

She smiled, an enigmatic smile, and inhaled the faint scent of the bouquet.

'Guns and roses,' she said. 'Now, how could I ever forget you?'

Writing on the Wall

THE WIND from the Thames buffeted the latticed window in the upper chamber of Beauchamp Tower. With a long, mournful wail it reverberated through the stone passages and down the spiral steps.

Crouched by the wall of his cell, the solitary figure took little notice, absorbed in the task he had begun at first light. The handle of the pewter spoon had become sharply pointed as he scraped away the stone particles to shape the letters he was carving. The task had taken longer than he had anticipated. A pewter spoon was a poor substitute for a mason's chisel, and the hard stone of the tower proved resistant to his efforts. It would take him a few more days to finish.

But even as he scraped the particles from the groove of the letter G of his name, the hollow echo of marching feet signalled that his time had run out.

For months he had lived in dread of this moment. Long days when the sweat streamed from every pore in his body as he lay on the straw pallet and thought of the agony that awaited him. Lonely nights when he desperately fought to control the suffocating fear that swelled within him and threatened to spill forth from his mouth in a despairing cry into the black silence. To carve the letters of his name on the prison wall was a frantic attempt to fill the empty but terrifying days of waiting. As the pewter spoon scraped away the particles to reveal each newly carved letter, a sense of determination, however, began to replace the dread, and the need to complete the letters of his name gradually became an obsessive compulsion.

As soon as the first glimmer of winter daylight crept through the slit window of his cell, he was on his knees by the wall, scrapping and fashioning. Every minute of his existence centred on the completion of the task he had set himself, to see his name, all sixteen letters of it, deface the stone of England's most prestigious and most feared fortress. An act of defiance, to leave some vestige of himself behind, as much as to prove to himself that he was capable of seeing at least one deed in his life through to the end. Because until now his life appeared as a litany of failures and unfulfilled promises, from personal relationships and political decisions to the last drastic collapse of his ill-timed revolt.

The sound of marching feet drew nearer. Feverishly he hacked away at the letter G in a vain attempt to complete what he knew would be the last act of his life. But a further five letters remained and, as the iron-studded door swung open, with it came the realisation that this, his last deed on earth, was to be as incomplete as his life. As if in final farewell to himself, he ran his fingers over the eleven letters he had finished, placed the misshapen spoon on the wooden table and turned around.

Framed in the doorway, the lieutenant of the Tower drew a parchment roll from a leather belt at his waist. Without ceremony, exuding an air of deliberate detachment, he read aloud his orders:

> *In the name of God and of his Sovereign Majesty
> the King, Thomas FitzGerald you have been found
> guilty of high treason for your crime of rebellion.
> You will be taken from hence to the
> place of execution at Tyburn where you are to be
> hanged by the neck. While still alive, your
> body will be taken down, disembowelled and
> quartered, so that no part of your person will
> remain intact as an affront to the King of*

this Realm of England.
Given under Our seal and signet this third day of
February, 1537.
Henry Rex

'God save the King,' the lieutenant concluded crisply.

Silence, broken by the crackling sound of the parchment as it snapped back into its cylindrical shape, greeted the grim details of the King's justice. Without further ado, the lieutenant turned quickly on his heel and left.

An armed guard of six halberdiers remained in the passage outside. Their captain entered the cell and signalled to the prisoner, who, in tattered hose and shirt, stood transfixed in the centre of the spartan cell.

Slowly the prisoner crossed to the window and from the ledge reached for his doublet of green velvet. It was soiled and crumpled. A silken fringe lay limply along the length of the sleeves, the silken fringe that had become synonymous with his name, *Tomás-an-tSioda*, Silken Thomas, in Ireland.

He remembered how vainly he had flaunted what had become his trademark in those first heady months of rebellion. His guard of forty mail-clad knights, friends and relations from the Pale, had all adopted the silken mark of their leader, with which they adorned their helmets and the trappings of their horses. What a glorious picture they had made, like King Arthur and his knights of old. To the ordinary people of the Pale, and even those in the Gaelic-held hinterland, he had, for that fleeting moment in time, fulfilled his destiny and become a hero.

'*Tomás-an-tSioda abu!*'

Even on the streets of that mongrel city Dublin – the loyalty of whose citizens, as he had found out to his cost, could be bought for the price of a loaf of bread – they had applauded and cheered him on.

'Long life to Silken Thomas.'

The thunderous eruption of his family's ancient war cry, *'Crom abu'*, from the throats of the be-rugged, long-haired Gaelic chieftains, and the doublet and bonneted lords of the Pale, massed before his family's great citadel, Maynooth Castle, had sent his blood pounding, energising his whole being. It was as if he was being towed on some gigantic, euphoric wave. He was fulfilling his destiny and for that space in time he had shone as brightly as any star in the firmament. He was the Messiah, come to lead his people from bondage. His name was on the lips of every chief and lord throughout the land. He had accomplished what his grandfather, the Great Earl of Kildare, and his father, for all their power and influence, had failed to do: to bring together the two disparate traditions in Ireland and bind them together in a single knot under his leadership.

O'Brien, O'Neill, O'Connor and MacMurrough, chiefs from Ireland's four provinces, Ulster, Munster, Connaught and Leinster, with Gaelic pedigrees as long as your arm, riding as one with the descendants of Anglo-Norman barons, Dunsany, Trimleston, Howth, Baltinglass and the rest. *Gael* and *Sean-Gall* united for the first time under the saltire of Kildare. The dream of generations of his ancestors, it seemed, through him, was about to be realised. He had trembled at the enormity of what he was about to do, praying that he would be worthy to shoulder the honour and the burden that had fallen to him.

He had worn the self-same fringed doublet, he recalled, under his armour, as a lucky omen, when on St Barnabas' Day he had set the wheels of his great rebellion in motion. In the vaulted chamber of St Mary's Abbey in Dublin, he had flung the Sword of State at the feet of the King's Council and boasted of his resolve to banish them and their Tudor master from Ireland forever.

And at first it looked as if he might succeed. His army had driven Henry's lackeys right up to the walls of Dublin and laid siege to the castle, while the King's Council cowered within. He had ravaged Ormond, the lordship of the pro-Tudor Butlers, the traditional enemies of his house. Even Gunner Skeffington, sent over by the King with great cannon and an army, had felt the brunt of his power at Clontarf and at Trim. Buoyed by his initial military success and the extravagant pledges of support from Henry's continental enemy, Charles V, he had imagined himself invincible, master of Ireland, impervious to the rule of the Tudor tyrant in England.

But his sense of invincibility had been his greatest failure, as much as had been his trust later in the King's offer of clemency. He had underestimated the Tudor appetite for revenge and had paid the price. Henry's offer of a deal had been nothing more than a lure to get him to England. He should have known that once a Tudor's claws became fixed on a Geraldine throat, nothing but death would loosen the grip. The hatred and the fear that existed between generations of Tudors and Geraldines ran far too deep. And now the outcome stared him implacably in the face.

The captain of the halberdiers shifted impatiently. Slowly the prisoner put on his doublet. He glanced through the window to the green below. His heart lurched inside him at the sight of his five uncles as they stood waiting in a line between two rows of guards. Henry Tudor's appetite for revenge would only be appeased by the blood of all living Geraldines.

Convulsively his hands tightened into fists of compressed hatred and frustration at his sense of helplessness to avert the fate intended for them all. But despairingly he knew that it was he and he alone who had presented the King, and the enemies of his house at the English court, with the opportunity they had long awaited: to annihilate the House of Kildare and with it the long-held ambition of his family to rule Ireland. The grand design, nourished by generations of Geraldines, had been eclipsed by his own intemperate actions.

In the end he knew he had been a poor match for the

duplicity of international politics, for the grim determination of Henry Tudor or for the disunity of his Irish allies, born out of centuries of ancient feuds and animosities. His rebellion had merely played into Henry Tudor's hands and provided him with the excuse he had always craved to eliminate the threat posed by the Geraldines to his rule in Ireland. How well the Tudor King had finally realised his ambition and how easy had been his victory in the end. With one final look at his unfinished epitaph on the wall, Thomas FitzGerald joined his armed escort.

The escort and their prisoner stepped through the narrow passageway, down the winding stairway of Beauchamp Tower and outside into the cold winter air. A crowd of onlookers, residents and workers in the tower stood gathered in a loose-knit bunch to witness another deputation being prepared for Tyburn. Since the King's break with Rome it had become a frequent occurrence; but since the Pilgrimage of Grace, every cell and black hole in the Tower was crammed to capacity with those awaiting a similar fate. Roman Catholic clerics, English nobles with vague claims to the English crown, anyone who wittingly or unwittingly invoked the King's anger, had met their end the same way. Irish rebels were more of a novelty. The son and five brothers of the King's one-time deputy in Ireland, about to be despatched at one fell swoop, was a spectacle too good to be missed.

Thomas embraced each of his uncles in turn: James, Walter, Richard, Oliver and John. There was nothing he could say in answer to the silent agony, the haunted look from deep-sunk eyes, that stared out from each pallid countenance. It had been a fearful wait these eighteen months, as their fate swung like a pendulum in the hands of the volatile King. Pardon or execution? The long-dreaded answer was now beyond doubt. And the knowledge that it was he who was responsible for what was to come had made the wait turn black with despair. For he knew that he had failed them ; lured them against their will into his rebellion with pledges of help from the emperor and the pope in Rome. But Spanish help had faltered at his inability to capture Dublin and had totally evaporated when Skeffington's cannon pounded Maynooth Castle into rubble. Charles V would waste no army on losers in Ireland. As for the pope, he should have known from history that Rome had never done Ireland any favours.

As he stood in line with his uncles he thought of his father. His gaze was momentarily drawn to the nearby outline of the chapel of St Peter-within-the-Tower, where the ninth earl of Kildare lay with More, Fisher, Anne Boleyn, all of them victims of the King's lust for revenge. Hopefully death had prevented his father from knowing how badly his son had failed him on each and every account that he had entrusted to him. His family about to end their days ignobly on the butcher's block. Maynooth Castle, the symbolic home of the FitzGeralds for four hundred years, now a gaunt ruin. The fertile lands of Kildare being fought over, like dogs over a carcass, by the King's rapacious officials and cronies in Ireland. The Geraldine saltire in tatters.

God's mercy that his father had been spared this day, he thought, as he closed his eyes in silent thanksgiving.

The sound of hooves and the clatter of wooden hurdles on the cobblestones heralded the arrival of their transport to Tyburn. On a curt order from the captain, the prisoners were spread-eagled and bound hand and foot to the hurdles. The portcullis of the Byward Tower was raised and the cortège issued forth over the muddied water of the moat, through the Lion Tower and into the city of London. The hurdles, bearing their doomed human cargo, bumped over the ruts and cobblestones.

The air of expectation among the onlookers along the way increased as the procession dragged its way up Tower Street into Cheapside, past St Paul's and into the Shambles. Through laneways and narrow streets, bordered by wooden-framed houses, taverns and shops, windows were thrown open and the contents of human and household waste were emptied down upon the bodies on the hurdles.

'Death to the rebels.'

'Pox on ye, Irish traitors.'

As hounds to the kill, the shouts of the excited citizenry increased at every corner in anticipation of the sordid spectacle about to be enacted.

Leaving the city walls through Newgate, the cortège moved slowly up Snow Hill, crossing the bridge over the Fleet river and on through the gardens and fields of Holborn.

As it arrived at Tyburn, a loud roar of approval issued from the mob assembled on the gallows field. Young and old, men and women, jostled to get a closer look at the prisoners as they were dragged through the crowd. Hundreds of faces, eyes feverish with expectation, mouths wide open, from which spewed forth streams of venomous abuse, looked down on the hapless victims. The hurdles halted beside a platform, dominated by a roughly hewn butcher's block. Alongside the platform was a gallows. The hemp noose swung ominously in the wind against the leaden sky.

The guards unhitched the hurdles and laid the prisoners side by side on the muddied grass. The crowd grew hushed as a huge hooded figure mounted the platform. A leather apron covered his clothes. From a box beneath the block the executioner removed the sinister tools of his trade.

A shudder ran through Thomas' body and a fearful trembling made him shake uncontrollably.

'Jesus Christ, help me,' he whispered.

'Courage, nephew. It will soon be over.' His uncle Walter, stretched alongside him on the grass, consoled him.

Great emotion welled inside Thomas. Despite his efforts tears began to roll freely down his face.

'Forgive me, uncle.'

With a smile Walter FitzGerald wearily nodded and closed his eyes. There was nothing more to be said.

The crowd was becoming restless. As the first victim was unbound and led to the scaffold, an exultant roar of approval rose into the air. Sir John FitzGerald was hoisted by the neck until his body jerked convulsively. The noose was removed from his neck with difficulty and he was placed lengthways on the block. A knife flashed and the executioner began his foul task.

Thomas closed his eyes, as if by doing so he could obliterate the hideous cries. The frenzied wails of pain rose and fell as the sharp knife cut through flesh and sinew. The executioner held aloft the first trophy to howls of delight from the crowd. He then employed a larger knife, which cut open the victim's abdomen. The cries reached an inhuman pitch, before gradually subsiding into animal-like whimpers, then finally into merciful silence. Piece by piece the dismembered body was flung into a large wooden receptacle under the platform until, with a final flourish, the head, grey hair matted with the victim's blood, was severed clean from the trunk. The executioner held high the grim proof of the completion of his task.

'God save the King,' he shouted.

'God save the King,' the mob howled in reply.

Five times the royal butcher held a Geraldine head aloft for the mob to bear witness.

By the time it was Thomas' turn to mount the scaffold, a strange numbness had spread through his body. The searing screams of his kinsmen, mingled with the clamour of the mob, had become somehow remote. As the rope cut into his neck and the breath was summarily ejected from his body, Thomas was only vaguely conscious of the pain and his own gasping efforts for air. The rope was jerked loose and his body crumpled to the wet boards. Hands seized him roughly and lay him on the execution block.

Through a red haze, a hooded face loomed above him. Through the slit holes of the hood, black eyes stared impassively into his. A flicker, maybe of pity, he could not be certain, flashed from the eyes above him. For a moment the bloodied hand that held the knife aloft hesitated. The prisoner closed his eyes.

Shielding the knife from the view of the crowd, the executioner inserted the lethal tool under the breastbone of the trembling body beneath him. With a sharp upward movement he sent his twenty-three-year-old victim to a swifter and more humane death than that ordained by the King.

For the sixth and final time the executioner went through the motions of the execution ritual. That the final victim did not cry out in agony like his predecessors went unnoticed by the now intoxicated mob, who continued to roar its approval at each stroke of the blade.

'God save the King.'

'God save the King.'

The golden-haired head of Silken Thomas FitzGerald, tenth earl of Kildare, tumbled into the wooden box in full and final retribution for the crime of rebellion against a king.

The body of Thomas FitzGerald was buried in the Priory of the Crutched (Crossed) Friars on Tower Hill. The King ordained that the heads and butchered quarters of his five uncles be dispersed throughout the city of London and displayed at various vantage points as a deterrent to would-be rebels.

In one of the recesses in the chilly state prison room in Beauchamp Tower, the unfinished epitaph, THOMAS FITZG, remains to this day a poignant reminder of a half-lived life.

Mad Carew

There's a green-eyed yellow idol to the north of Kathmandu.
There's a little marble cross below the town.
There's a broken-hearted women tends the grave of Mad Carew,
While the little god forever gazes down.

J. MILTON HAYES

IS SOBRIQUET, Mad Carew, had been earned for his exploits on the battlefield. Since his very first engagement, some sixteen years ago, at the bugle's first notes a surge of blood would course through his body to launch him headlong into the fray, as if a stick of gelignite or a powerful Chinese cracker had exploded within him.

With a sabre in one hand, a revolver in the other, his knees directing his horse in the mad gallop, stop and start of hand-to hand combat, his tally of enemy bodies in every engagement doubled that of his fellow officers. He dared not look at whom he shot through or cleaved open with his blade. That way there were no terrified or beseeching eyes to disturb his sleep at night. The butchery was done in some vacuum, where all his senses seemed to have become suspended. He did not hear the cries of the wounded. He did not feel the blade cut through flesh and sinew, nor see bare bones protruding from the crimson gash, nor smell the sickly odour of fresh blood oozing from the lifeless bodies that lay on the red dust, mangled under the hooves of his horse. He slashed and shot his way through the brown-skinned ranks, Muslim and Hindu, Sikh, Afghan, Mahratta and Rajput, like one possessed by some demonic force that drove him on and would give him no respite until the battle was fought and won.

His subalterns had coined his nickname 'Mad Carew' both as a tribute to his reckless intensity in battle and an uneasy suspicion as to the soundness of his mind when the blood-lust took control of him. But it also was in recognition of the charismatic side of Tom Carew that made them gravitate towards him, seek out his company, want to become his friend. To the rank and file he was a hero. To the native *sepoy* recruits, despite the colour of his skin and his rank, he was one of them.

They followed him unquestionably in the certain knowledge that whatever he ordered them to do was no more than he would do himself. Their respect was enhanced with an affectionate devotion to him for the easy familiarity with which he treated them. He was as often to be found around the campfires in the native lines, sharing their *badjeree*, as in the British barracks. His fraternising with the native troops, crossing over the strict social and racial boundaries between white and coloured ranks, ran contrary to the mores of Empire. But army command turned a blind eye, aware that his popularity with the native troops and their absolute loyalty to him served the Empire's interests where it most counted, on the battlefield.

To his fellow officers he was the ideal club man, able to hold his drink and his manners. He was a gambler, who pushed the pot to its limits but who never reneged on a bet made or a debt owed; the prankster who spiced up the monotony of barrack life with his tricks and escapades; the dare-devil *shakira*, to whose gun and spear tiger and wild boar fell more than seemed natural, leading the natives to wonder and endow him with some magical power. He was the entertainer who could enliven the mess on the sultry, sticky nights before the monsoon with tales and stories of army life, so humorously outlandish that they could not have possibly been invented and therefore must be, as he claimed, true. He was the lyric tenor who, when the mood took him, by his rendition of the songs of Thomas Moore, could make the fresh, green, dew-tipped fields of Ireland and England appear like some mirage and dispel the dust-bowl bareness of their sweltering surroundings. For a brief moment, his voice made campaign-hardened men grow silent as home sickness and emotion threatened to break through their army-instilled reserve.

The physique that encompassed such a daring and charismatic character was not, as might be supposed, one of heroic proportions. At thirty-six, well built in a solid, uncompromising way, Carew was no more than of medium height. Dark brown hair, a fair complexion, a regular face with no apparent distinguishing features – straight nose, average forehead, solid chin – displayed no outward indication of anyone out of the ordinary. Perhaps his eyes, dark blue with a fleck of amber, which could flash just as quickly in anger as in merriment, could be said to be his most arresting feature. But it was the totality of his well-proportioned physique, and the essence of unpredictability that he exuded, like a spring ready to uncoil, that set him apart and made men walk cautiously around him.

Among themselves the men in his squad likened him to the very tiger that he often stalked, unpredictable and dangerous, not to be trifled with. Since his transfer to the British enclave in Nepal, with no military campaign on which to expend his explosive energy, it was like waiting for a geyser to boil over. And with the arrival of Miss Elizabeth Hodgson, boil over it did.

His fellow officers knew little about Carew's background, other than what they gleaned from the occasional off-hand remark he made when, during a game of bridge, or as they sipped their whiskey and sodas before tiffin, talk of home surfaced.

He was of farming stock in Ireland. His family were possessed of sufficient acres and means to afford him a good education. As a younger son, with no claim to anything, his prospects were limited and his life in Ireland aimless, centred as it was around hunting, racing and carousing. When the girl whom he had idolised, with the same passionate intensity that he later expended on his military exploits, deserted him for his more eligible older brother, he had drifted into the army. Through the influence of the local lord-of-the-manor he had secured a commission and a place at the military college at Addiscombe, near Croydon. From there he had been sent for active service to India.

For the first time in his life Carew had found his niche. Army service suited him. Its boundaries and structures gave his life some purpose. The comradeship of his fellow soldiers filled the lonely void within him. The action and adventure that was the hallmark of the army of the Raj in India was the bonus. And he had already seen his share of action: from the burning desert sands of Rajastan, to the snow-topped mountain tracks of the North West Frontier and in the vast emptiness of the Gangetic plain, before his banishment to the remote mountain-top kingdom of Nepal.

Many nights as he smoked a cigar after dinner he looked out to where the gigantic Himalayan peaks in the distance speared the darkening sky to the east. Then the feeling of abandonment in the vast isolation of his backward garrison post, in this remote eyrie near the top of the world, made the anger rise inside him as to the reason why. Nepal made him feel as if he had been left suspended in mid-air, somewhere between heaven and earth.

He was a soldier not a politician and to him racism stopped at the army gate. It made little difference in the heat of battle if your fellow soldier was brown or white-skinned. There were brave white soldiers and brave brown ones; there were brown cowards and white cowards. The arrogant eyes of the major, newly arrived from England, had flickered in surprise at his intervention, before recoiling as Carew's fist had crashed into his face. The *sepoy* whom the major had just kicked down the stairs of the officer's mess, for the 'confounded nigger's' temerity of knocking on the mess door at dinner, had put out a placating hand to stop him. He knew well the consequences of his captain's intervention. The moment his fist had crashed into the insolent white face Carew knew that his army career had ground to a halt. The top brass had not appreciated an officer taking the side of a native against a fellow officer, not to mention the son of an influential family back in England.

Carew's punishment had been banishment to Nepal, to Kakani to be exact, the outpost of Empire, and to a life of monotonous inaction. His job was merely one of glorified babysitting the British Resident. Nepal was not within the ambit of the Empire, but an obscure treaty earlier in the century had given Britain a toehold in the mountainous kingdom. The British base was a strategic hill-top station, a few miles north of the royal city of Kathmandu. Commanding an encompassing view of the city and the valley below, Kakani was the Empire's eye on Nepal, which it held with a small military detachment, mainly cavalry, comprising a hundred officers and men and a few additional ancillary services. There were no battles or military engagements to employ Carew's energy, nothing to break the monotony of each day other than the daily drill and ceremonial salute before the Resident's bungalow on the *maidan*.

His posting, he had long concluded, was as empty as the British presence in this fiercely independent mountain kingdom: a sham, a miserable excuse for living. As he saluted the raising and lowering of the flag at dawn and dusk each day, this sense of living in a vacuum became increasingly acute. The British contingent were merely tolerated by Nepal's aristocratic rulers. Confined to Kakani and the surrounding valley, they were kept in virtual isolation by their Nepalese hosts, who were often overtly resentful and ever suspicious of their presence. They were merely policemen, spies, sending their reports on whatever could be gleaned about the machinations of the various Nepalese factions in Kathmandu back to headquarters in Delhi. Their presence, Carew knew, was merely at the whim of their reluctant hosts, who, if they took the notion, could easily have them expelled or massacred.

To the south-west the ancient brick and wooden city of Kathmandu, rose like a citadel from out of the valley below. At dawn, when the morning sun rose from behind the shimmering peaks to the east, in the pale, tea-rose sky, the city was bathed in a burnt-peach hue. For a time it camouflaged the decay and filth that became cruelly exposed as the fierce sun rose higher in the cloudless sky.

For Carew the arrival of the colonel's daughter from England that spring had changed everything. From the moment he had heard her laughter, as she fell out of the palanquin that had conveyed her from Patna to the Nepalese border, Carew had been smitten. The monotony of his posting, the boredom that had enveloped his being, had suddenly evaporated like the wisps of vapour that he had often seen rising from the frozen peaks in the distance. From the moment he had taken her hand to help her up from the muddy ground, it was as if he had made contact with some magnetic force that bound him fast.

Two green-blue eyes looked up nonchalantly into his and a smile parted her lips.

'Have I landed in India or Nepal?'

'On the borders, ma'am,' he replied stiffly, still discomposed by the feelings that surged inside him.

'Oh dear, not a good first impression, but blame the mode of transport – it made me seasick,' she laughed unconcernedly as she looked at the detachment of soldiers drawn up at a distance.

'Captain Thomas Carew.' He saluted. 'I am to escort you through Kathmandu and …'

'There is something of a musical ring to that, wouldn't you say, Captain?' she interrupted. 'You could sing it, and, I daresay, you have a fine singing voice too.'

'... And from there to the Residency at Kakani,' he continued, feeling totally foolish.

She was young, about twenty at the most, he reckoned, and lovely. Her face was pale and oval in shape. Her head, which was covered loosely in a blue silk scarf wound around in native fashion, from which auburn tresses spilled out, came above his shoulder. A pearl-grey dress, buttoned to the neck, accentuated the outline of her figure. Two mischief-filled, observant eyes noted and seemed pleased by his discomfiture.

'So, how am I to get to Kathmandu, Captain Carew?' she said, emphasising the rhyming syntax.

Behind him he heard his men snigger.

'To Kakani,' he corrected her. 'And, since you seem to have parted company with the palanquin, may I suggest the baggage cart.' He looked at her severely, hoping that by doing so it might restore his composure.

'I can ride with your men.' She moved over to where his detachment sat mounted, awaiting his orders, and smiled at them.

From where he stood Carew could see the effect she had on them as, to a man, they straightened up in the saddle, eyes bright with expectation.

She turned back towards him. 'Just in case I fall off again.'

The company smothered their laughter.

'I'm afraid that the British cavalry does not provide side-saddles.' He could kick himself for how officious, even prissy, he sounded, but she had knocked him for six.

'Don't you think I know that, Captain Carew? I am the daughter of a soldier. Army regulation is good enough for me.' She smiled broadly at his men.

He shrugged and motioned to his corporal to have her bags placed in the waiting oxen cart. A spare horse was lead forward and a wooden crate was brought into position as a substitute mounting block. The combined eyes of his detachment were fixated and rewarded by the flash of a slim leg as she nimbly swung herself into the saddle. She rearranged her dress and tightened the silk scarf around her head.

'That's more like it.' She breathed deeply. 'At least I can see where I'm going. How far to this Kakani,' she asked him as he mounted his horse alongside.

'Forty miles, ma'am.'

She sighed. 'That long. Well, at least I can look forward to your company, Captain, to shorten the way.'

He looked into her laughing eyes, which seemed both to mock and, at the same time, entice him. She was a handful, he suspected, but a handful he was more than willingly to endure.

The colonel had hinted as much when he had appointed him to lead the detachment to accompany his daughter from the border.

'I simply have no idea what I am to do with her here in Nepal, of all places. It's no place for a woman. But I have little choice. Her education in England is completed and, with her mother dead, there was simply nowhere else she could go.'

'I'm sure she'll fit in, sir,' he had said diplomatically. He found his commanding officer to be fair-minded if somewhat lack-lustre, who like himself took his posting to Nepal as a demotion and, in his case, a place of rest until his retirement.

'Fit in? You do not know my daughter, Carew. Fitting in is not in Elizabeth's nature. She will have me and the entire cantonment in a spin. Believe me.'

'Maybe that's what this place needs.'

Colonel Hodgson looked at him from under his bushy eyebrows and grunted. 'It's bad enough as it is.'

'How is my father?'

'The colonel is very well, ma'am,' Carew replied as he led his detachment along the rocky trail that led upwards towards the hills.

In the damp sweltering heat of the Tarai he could feel the sweat roll down inside his heavy uniform. He looked across at the colonel's daughter but she seemed unaffected, sitting straight in the saddle, cool and poised, as if it were a Sunday morning ride in Hyde Park.

'Can you not call me by my name, Elizabeth? Ma'am makes me feel so old, so ... sensible.'

He looked at her and smiled. 'One could not accuse you of either.'

'Well, Captain, I will take the first as a compliment.'

'The colonel is, ah ... looking forward to seeing you.'

'My father is terrified at the prospect of my arrival.'

He could not help but laugh.

'You should do that more often, Captain. Laughter is good for the soul, or so we were told by the nuns in my convent. You're Irish?'

He nodded.

'There were Irish nuns in the convent and, to tell you the truth, I liked them best. So I expect I will like you best in the regiment.'

'Then I will take that as a compliment.'

'As it is intended.' Her eyes flirted wickedly with his and Carew felt his heart pound.

As her father had predicted, the entire British cantonment, from the mess to the barracks, were bit by bit turned on their heads by his daughter's arrival. Apart from the wife of the station surgeon, and the elderly sister of the army chaplain, there were no other white women in the cantonment. Certainly no one as young, as beautiful and as vital as Elizabeth.

Down in the valley the families of the British traders visited the enclave but rarely, on special occasions to celebrate the Queen's birthday, Christmas and such like. Other than that the soldiers and officials of the garrison saw little in the way of female company, officially at least. Unofficially, although camp followers and prostitutes were less numerous in Nepal than in

India, desires among the soldiers generally found a native outlet.

From the start, Elizabeth flitted and flirted her way throughout the cantonment. From her father's bungalow, the mess, the barracks, even the native lines, all came within her orbit. Her friendliness and curiosity, which bordered on naivety, seemed to bring out the best in officers and men alike. She was a delicious diversion to the boredom of the daily routine. Nothing was too much trouble when it induced a smile or a word from her lips. Every subaltern would have gladly killed the other to be the one to sit opposite her at table when she came with her father each Sunday to dine at the officers' mess. Her presence on the reviewing stand at the daily muster made the men parade with renewed precision.

To the *sepoys* and their families living in the native quarters, at a remove from the all-white cantonment, the visits of the *memsahib* Elizabeth to their flimsy dwellings was the source of much pride and pleasure. From officer, to trooper, to *sepoy*, Carew saw the spell she cast on all who came into contact with her and a curious jealousy began to grow inside him, catching him unawares.

Since coming to India, he had little inclination to become involved again with any of the women who had crossed his path. A brief affair with the wife of a political agent, who had reminded him of the woman he had once loved in Ireland, had been his only foray back into the complicated world of lust and love. Unlike most of his comrades, he had rarely succumbed to the charms of the *bibis* in the native brothels, his fear of disease being for him a greater deterrent than any moral scruple. He had been content to live in his all-male world of the barracks, the mess and the parade ground; whiskey, cigars, cards, the smell of horses and the crude talk of men.

When desires kicked in, where once there had been action in the field in the Indian campaigns, now the occasional tiger-shoot and pig-sticking offered some relief. There was a belief throughout the service, and it was one to which Carew sub-scribed, that the danger, the ferocity, the sheer excitement attained from hunting wild boar, armed only with a primitive spear, was an essential outlet for the pent-up emotions that simmered within men confined to barracks, restricted to much the same company and, for the most part, without an outlet to appease their sexual appetite. Carew had speared more than his share of wild boar.

But Elizabeth's arrival had stirred up latent memories of the obverse of his all male-oriented life: the scent of perfume and of flowers, the swish of a long dress, the clink of china at afternoon tea, the chatter and sense of anticipation and unpre-dictability that female company inspired. Meeting her, the emotions that he had buried deep inside him had begun to sur-face. And he had good reason to suppose that, despite the openness and friendliness with which she seemed to treat everyone else in the camp, she reserved something more for him, that somehow he was special to her.

She looked for him on the parade, her eyes sending him some secret message across the massed ranks. She often wait-ed for him in the shade, as he dismissed his squad, so that he could walk her back to the bungalow. The sparring at their ini-tial meeting at the border continued. Added to it was some-thing more, something that had begun to grow inside him the very moment he had set eyes on her and something he hoped was beginning to be felt by her as well. She had started to ask questions about his background in Ireland, his army career in India. Gently but determinedly she had probed emotions and feelings of the past that he had cast from his mind. With her he began to feel as if the side of him that had become as frozen as the perennial snow-cap on the distant Himalayan peaks was beginning to thaw and make him whole again.

When Elizabeth finally tired of the restrictive limits of the British cantonment, they were thrown together even more.

Carew had received a summons to the colonel's office. As

he crossed the barrack square, he took off his helmet to mop his brow, wet from the exertions of drill in the soaring May temperatures. He wondered if the old man had called him in for a dressing-down regarding his friendship with Elizabeth.

Already his comrades had begun to chaff him at the apparent place he had captured in the affections of the colonel's daughter.

'You're in there big time, Carew. The Irish charm is working a treat.'

'Never thought of you as much of a ladies' man, old boy. How wrong can you be?'

'But will he be able to handle her? There is a wild streak in her that needs some taming.'

'With all the tigers Carew has bagged, it will be a cake walk, eh, Carew?'

At first he had laughed off their comments, rebuffed their jibes with accusations of jealousy. But as his feelings for Elizabeth had become more intense, by the way his eyes flicked with unfriendly fire, they knew not to taunt him any more. Among themselves they whispered that Mad Carew had it bad and had been brought to heel by the young Englishwoman. But silently every man among them cursed his own luck, that it was not him who had been singled out by the colonel's daughter for special attention, and envied Carew his luck.

'Elizabeth informs me that she has tired of the cantonment,' the colonel said with resignation, as he indicated that Carew take a seat.

Carew breathed easier. Elizabeth had been cajoling him along a similar vein all of the past week and he had not discouraged her, in the hope that he might be able to spend more time with her. Even as it was, she filled his every waking moment as well as his dreams.

'Finds it claustrophobic, no less. Hmph. If she had to spend two years here like you and I, Carew, she might have something to complain about, eh? Wants to spread her wings, she says. See Kathmandu, no less. God knows why. There's little to see, as we know. The bloody place is a veritable dunghill.'

'Perhaps it's the weather, sir. Being confined in these temperatures. For one not fully acclimatised, it must be trying. Some sightseeing, early morning and late evening to avoid the heat, might break the monotony. The pagodas and temples, as you know, are quite interesting.'

'You sound as if you are talking yourself into a chaperone's job, Carew.'

'I will be happy to oblige, sir.'

'Well, at least you have the experience, in case of any danger. You do realise our limitations here. We are merely tolerated. Any transgressions would put the British position in jeopardy, not to mention my pension.'

'I am aware of the limitations, sir.'

The colonel nodded and looked at him from beneath his brows.

'And I trust you know your limitations regarding my daughter, Captain.'

'Your daughter will be safe with me, sir.'

With a few armed guards as escort, Carew and Elizabeth set out as the dawn was lighting up the gigantic peaks to the east for the journey towards the old city in the valley below. They started initially with the area of Kathmandu around the *Hanuman Dhoka*, the royal palace, a tight tangle of narrow alleys to the north and south of the city, adorned with a multitude of temples, shrines and monuments to every known god and goddess in the Nepalese calendar – Hindu, Buddhist and Shaman.

'There is a god or a goddess for everything and everyone in Nepal,' Carew explained to a wide-eyed Elizabeth. 'No one is left out, from the manure sweeper to the king, everyone has his own personal deity to look after his welfare.'

'Some better than others,' Elizabeth said, pointing to where two old women, bowed down under their bundles of dried wood, slowly made their way along the cobbles.

'There are many worse off, believe me. As you can see, the city is a series of unending shrines.'

It was early morning and the air was still fresh and not yet polluted with the worst excess of the open sewers, manure and household rubbish that lay strewn along the narrow streets and lanes, which, in the boiling temperatures of mid-day, made the city unbearable. The streets had not quite filled with the pulsating, noisy traffic of daytime.

Carew showed her Kathmandu's oldest building, the *Kasthamandap*, an open pagoda-roofed pavilion, considered to be the oldest wooden building in the world, and the *Kumari Chowk*, the gilded temple of Kathmandu's living goddess.

'A living goddess? Shame on you, Tom Carew, you are telling tall tales,' Elizabeth upbraided him, her face registering her disbelief.

'I swear it is true. A young girl is chosen from among the caste of goldsmiths by the elders and is deemed a goddess, until such time as she grows up and becomes a woman. Then another girl is chosen in her place, and so it goes on. Until she grows up she lives in seclusion, shut away here in the *Kumari Chowk*, seldom seen in public, except on special feast days.'

'What a terrible life. I think I'd rather be just plain, ordinary me,' Elizabeth said.

They watched the people doing their daily religious rituals at their favourite shrines and temples. Many of the shrines were gold-clad, some decorated with precious and semi-precious gems. To appease or venerate their chosen idol, the devotees adorned it with tokens of their homage, from a covering of gaudy red paste, to flower garlands and rice. From inside the Buddhist temples the melodious chanting of the monks and the tinkle of the ceremonial bells wafted through the morning air.

By the time the sun had climbed skywards to reveal the stench and squalor of Kathmandu, Carew knew it was time to leave. The crush and clamour of humanity now filled every space, as hawkers, drovers, water-carriers, porters, pilgrims, priests, goats, cows, dogs and the ever-present impudent monkeys jostled along the herring-boned, paved medieval streets. Swarms of mosquitoes, mites, fleas and lice began to bite and made it doubly unbearable. Elizabeth was more than agreeable to escape back to the relative calm and order of Kakani.

'It's been like a dream, as if I stepped into another world. I cannot wait to see the rest of it,' Elizabeth said as he helped her dismount in a shady corner of the *maidan*.

He held her hand for a moment longer than was necessary. She made no effort to release it.

'And you made it even more special, Tom. In fact you are special.'

She said it without the bantering tone that she habitually used when anything vaguely personal arose between them. He felt his heart race in anticipation.

'I'm glad you think so,' he said and raised her hand to his lips. 'Because I was going to tell you that you are special to me.'

For the first time he sensed that she was the one at a disadvantage. She smiled uncertainly at him, mumbled something about an appointment and hurried away. He watched her across the *maidan*. At the steps to the veranda of the colonel's bungalow she turned and looked back at him. He raised his stick to his helmet in salute and watched as she disappeared into the shadows.

Over the succeeding weeks, Carew revelled in his job as Elizabeth's escort. He watched her reaction to the sights, both wondrous and appalling, felt her hand reach for his when crowds of natives, men, women and children, jostled to view her more closely.

'They are just curious,' he reassured her. 'They think you

are as strange looking as you do them. They mean no harm. Just smile and look ahead.'

'Nobody looked twice at me in India.'

'Then the Nepalese have better taste.'

She smiled at him. 'And you, Captain Carew. Am I to your taste?'

He looked at her. Her eyes neither mocked nor teased him, just awaited his response. He took her hand and raised it to his lips and, without moving his eyes from hers, he kissed her fingers.

'You are the most desirable woman I have ever met.'

She seemed to weigh up his words, as if considering whether they measured up to what she wanted or expected to hear him say. She smiled wickedly.

'Well, coming from you, Captain Carew, a man of the world, a man of some experience, I'll be bound, I daresay I must be satisfied with that.'

Before he could pursue the conversation and let her know how he truly felt about her, she had whirled around towards the next sight. He followed her slowly.

He must be patient, he told himself, not scare her off. Take every step with care, like when he tracked the tiger through the twisting ravines and gullies. Although she acted and talked as if she was experienced in relationships, she was as naive as could be expected from a convent-reared girl. She was young, impressionable but, like the tiger, also unpredictable. Carew resolved to tread with caution.

But Carew's intentions of slowly pursuing Elizabeth were thwarted by circumstances outside his control. The arrival in the cantonment at the end of May of the Honourable Jeremy Woodford increased the pace of the chase to capture Elizabeth's affections, as well as raising Carew's ardour to boiling point.

On his first sighting of the newcomer at a reception in the

Resident's house, Carew immediately sensed the danger: the tall, handsome aristocrat was captivated by Elizabeth. Through the drawing-room window, he watched them converse on the veranda outside. In a blue silk dress, her hair tied back from her face, Elizabeth looked her loveliest and most animated self, seemingly oblivious to the admiring glances the Englishman gave her. But Carew noted the newcomer's interest and resolved to register his claim to Elizabeth's affections before things between them had a chance to progress any further.

'Tom, do come and meet Jeremy. He has all the latest gossip from England. It's better than having your own postal delivery.' Elizabeth gave a laugh and turned in mock apology to her companion. 'I hope you don't mind being my postman?'

'I will settle for being your postman any time, Miss Hodgson.'

They chatted together for a while. The Resident, Woodford informed Carew, had been a school chum of his father and had invited him to Nepal.

'His Excellency was telling me last evening at supper that you are a *shakira* of some expertise, Captain. Tiger your speciality, I believe. Perhaps I could accompany you on your next outing?'

'I'm afraid Nepal is no place for novices. The terrain here is too treacherous.'

Elizabeth looked at Carew, surprised by the tone of his response. Silently he cursed his words. He had not meant to sound so priggish and felt a fool. In contrast to him, Woodford seemed to possess all the confidence and *sang froid* of the English aristocratic order. At ease with himself, he spoke with the confident air of someone with nothing to prove, sure of his place and position in life. He was witty, disarming and surprisingly pleasant-mannered. In contrast, Carew felt ill-at ease and all buttoned-up, as if he was about to explode inside his uniform. Accustomed as he was to orders and regularity, it was difficult at times to project the person inside the uniform, and this was one of those times. On his own with Elizabeth, he felt, by contrast, at ease and in control.

With Woodford's arrival, Carew's intimate sorties with Elizabeth outside the cantonment, and his plans to pursue her affections, received a set-back. Their morning excursions now included the newcomer.

'But Tom, you know so much about everything here, the temples, the pagodas, the burning ghats, and Jeremy is so anxious to see it all. I had to insist that he come too. You don't mind, do you?'

The blue eyes looked pleadingly into his and he could do little but shrug, while inside he felt his frustration veer towards a boiling anger.

As he retraced what he and Elizabeth had already seen together, Carew began to feel more and more that he was merely the guard and guide to a couple who seemed to become more intimate as the days went by. He became sullen and withdrawn and imparted his knowledge to them brusquely.

'Oh, please, do tell Jeremy about the living goddess and the *Kumari Chowk*, Tom.'

To please her he recounted the story again for Woodford's amusement and was rewarded by a warm smile and a whisper from Elizabeth.

'There, I told him you were the best guide in Kathmandu and you have proved me right.'

She looped her arm through his as she used to do before Woodford's arrival and Carew felt the warm glow that her touch induced spread through his body.

'Does he have to come everywhere with us?'

'How else can Jeremy see all the sights? I cannot show him on my own. Father would have a fit. You know everything about everything, Tom, and besides,' she squeezed his arm, 'I like having the two most handsome men in the cantonment at my beck and call.'

Her eyes danced with wicked humour. Woodford strolled

towards them and Elizabeth linked her other arm in his.

'It's stifling here. I know, let's go and see the shrine of the little idol, in that village down in the valley, the one you told me about, Tom.'

'Its too far in this heat.'

'What a killjoy you've become. Then we'll wait until evening, when the heat has lessened. We can ride there, the three of us.'

'What a splendid idea,' Woodford concurred.

'As non-residents, we are under restrictions as to where we can go.' Carew glared at his rival.

'Forgive me, Captain, I had no wish to compromise your position.'

'Oh, tish. You both make it sound as if we were going to the moon. I will ask Father.'

Woodford smiled indulgently at Elizabeth and then, with a shrug, threw a look of exasperation at Carew.

'Looks like neither of us has a choice in the matter, old man.'

Elizabeth got her way as Carew knew she would. As the long shadows of evening lengthened and the heat of the day lessened, with a small company of cavalry, the next day Carew led the party northwards from the cantonment. They made slow progress along the narrow, rocky track, busy with oxen carts, ambling water buffalo, yaks, elephants, rickshaws, innumerable cows and women and men bent double under their heavy loads. The air was heavy with the scent of chir pine and chestnut, as the trail snaked its way down into a sub-tropical valley, fertile and verdant.

A few miles from Kakani, Carew led them off the main track, through wooded countryside and past a ramshackle village. A mile further on they dismounted and Carew beckoned Elizabeth and Woodford to follow him along a narrow goat track, bordered by a stream that leaped and gurgled its way over the rocks and stones. The track opened into a clearing dominated by a solitary chir pine to reveal a stone grotto containing a small yellow idol. Behind him Carew heard Elizabeth gasp.

'Oh, how divine.'

In contrast to the shrines in Kathmandu, with their ornate and gilded decorations and overpowering smell of incense, this was breathtaking in its sheer simplicity. It was as if the god had ordained that, as nature had endowed his grotto so perfectly, humans need do no more. Rhododendron bushes, laden with blooms of the richest vermilion and of the softest pink, provided a canopy to the little god. Tree ferns, of lush green, stretched out their tentacles in supplication. Alongside a stream provided music as evocative as the haunting sound of native *bansuri* or the tinkle of temple bells, while, all around, the sweet smell of wild orchids provided the incense. The atmosphere evoked a complete sense of peace and contemplation. Elizabeth spoke in a whisper.

'What god is it, Tom?'

'It is a manifestation of the great god, *Mahadev*. The people of the village we passed through rely on him to provide them with a good harvest each year and to protect their animals.'

Elizabeth stood transfixed before the idol

'Look at his eyes. They seem to follow one everywhere.'

Woodford stepped closer to the idol. 'By Jove! Real emeralds, I'd say.'

'Emeralds?'

Elizabeth reached up towards the idol to see for herself.

'Don't. Don't touch it.'

Carew's angry shout made her freeze.

'I say, old man, steady on, no need to shout,' Woodford rebuked him.

'There's every need, if you want to leave the village alive.' Carew turned towards Elizabeth. 'I'm sorry, Elizabeth, but the idol is considered sacred by the villagers, out of bounds, particularly to us.'

'I didn't mean any harm.'

'It wasn't as if she was going to pinch the emeralds, Carew, though I'm surprised they have remained intact out here in this wilderness. They are beauties.'

'It's as if they can see inside to your soul.' Elizabeth shivered

'Maybe that is why they have remained so long where they are,' Carew said. 'Come on, it's time we were heading back.'

They spoke little on the return journey. Elizabeth scarcely looked in Carew's direction. He sensed her aloofness but Woodford's presence prevented him from speaking to her in the more intimate way he used to when they were on their own. When they dismounted before her father's bungalow, she hurried inside without a word.

'See you at dinner, Elizabeth,' Woodford called after her. He nodded amiably to Carew then walked across the square towards his quarters.

In the descending gloom, as Carew headed for his own quarters, the jealousy and anger gnawed a hole inside him.

Elizabeth's glumness did not last long. Within a day or two, she had restored Carew to his place in her orbit. But now that she had become accustomed to having two admirers vie for her company, her womanly vanity could not allow her relinquish either. For what she lacked in experience of men, Elizabeth more than made up for in female instinct. The sense of power, as well as the excitement, accorded her in having two suitors in thrall, she found addictive. But neither Carew nor Woodford saw the game she played with them. Each of them merely saw the other as an opponent, an obstacle to be overcome, to win her exclusive affection for themselves.

To have to share Elizabeth with Woodford, the outsider, the interloper, was beginning to become as unbearable to Carew as the humidity and energy-sapping heat that heralded the monsoon period. Realistically he knew he fought a rear-guard action. Because of his privileged position as a personal friend of the Resident, as well as his aristocratic status, Woodford enjoyed an access to Elizabeth not open to Carew. He was her companion at the Resident's dinner table, at the musical evenings arranged by the chaplain's sister and the numerous bridge and whist parties confined to the Residency staff and the army top brass. Because of Woodford's background and prospects as heir to his father's estate, his suitability as a suitor for Elizabeth's affections, from a material point of view, were vastly more attractive, Carew well realised, than his own.

With a growing sense of hopelessness he knew how little he had to offer her by comparison. His prospects in the army were, for the time being at least, uncertain. His future outside the army was non-existent. His only consolation in his pursuit of Elizabeth was that Woodford could not stay in Nepal indefinitely. The monsoon season was drawing near and transient people, like Woodford, usually departed before the rain, mud and landslides made it impossible. He and Elizabeth were scheduled to remain for the long haul, provided, of course, that Woodford's obvious attraction to her was not reciprocated in the meantime. All he could do, Carew rationalised, was to keep as close to her as his duties and propriety allowed, and thereby give his rival as little chance as possible to pursue her affections and turn them into something more enduring.

But Woodford showed little inclination to leave. When Elizabeth made her announcement a few days later, with a heavy heart Carew realised that his rival was destined to remain in Kakani longer than he had hoped.

'Well, I simply must tell you two gentlemen before everyone else. I am to be twenty-one next week. My father is resolved to celebrate this great event in the calendar of mankind with a ball, right here in the cantonment.'

They were sitting on the veranda of her father's bungalow. Carew had walked Elizabeth back from the barrack square after morning drill. They had no sooner sat on the veranda than they were joined by Woodford.

'Well, my dear Elizabeth, I promise you that we will all endeavour to make it memorable, isn't that so, Carew?'

Carew did not respond. If things had been different and he had been allowed to pursue Elizabeth without the newcomer's interference, he knew how he would have made her birthday special. By asking her to marry him. He saw Woodford take Elizabeth's hand and raise it to his lips. At that moment, instinctively, Carew knew that his rival was thinking along similar lines.

'I have two gifts already in mind for your special birthday, Elizabeth,' he heard Woodford say. 'One, I have already decided upon. The other, you must choose yourself.'

'Jeremy, you make me blush. Just as well Father is out of earshot.'

'Come, you must let me know what you most want in the world and, by hell or high water, I promise I will get it for you.'

'Be careful what you promise, otherwise I might ask for something quite impossible,' Elizabeth joked.

'I told you, anything.'

'Well then, you asked for it. Nothing else will do save a green eye of the little yellow God, the one we saw the other day in that heavenly grotto.'

Woodford's face noticeably blanched.

'Look, Tom, how positively pale he has turned,' Elizabeth said, delighting in Woodford's apparent unease. 'That will teach you to make promises you cannot keep,' she mocked.

'Well, anything other than the eye of a god then. Will another emerald not do?'

'See, your devotion to me has its limits after all. I bet if I had asked Tom here, he would not balk as you do.'

Woodford turned around to face his rival.

'I imagine that Captain Carew knows his limitations.'

There was both a challenge and an insult implicit in

Woodford's tone that made Carew's blood boil. Elizabeth saw his eyes flash with anger and rose quickly.

'This weather makes us all silly. I hope the rains will not come and spoil my party.'

Woodford smiled at her, pleasant-mannered and poised again. 'They would not dare.'

The rains did not dare to make their appearance, but the heat and humidity did their utmost to dampen the atmosphere and sap the energy of those involved in preparing for the great event, the social highlight of the season. The entire cantonment, rank and file, was to attend an open-air feast to be held on the barrack-square. Afterwards the officers were to attend a ball in the Residency. Invitations were sent post-haste down to the British station at Patna, to the officials and their families in the British cantonment there and to the British traders and their families living in the valley.

As the temperatures soared, the heat and humidity made tempers flare. In the barracks after morning drill, the men lounged in whatever shade they could find or lay lank and sweating on their narrow beds, amid the foul smell of body odour and leaking latrines, ill-trimmed kerosene lamps and stale tobacco.

In his room Carew suffered like the rest. But his body was wracked not only by the weather but by a dark and dangerous thought that had begun to form in his mind and which made the sweat ooze from every pore in his body and his heart pound in dread.

What he contemplated, he knew, made his previous madcap escapades, his daring exploits in battle and skirmish, the life-threatening risks he had taken, when the amber-flecked eyes of the wounded tiger had burned into his before springing at him in a final bound of death, all pale into nothing. What he contemplated was not war, nor a prank, not even an escapade. It went against orders, loyalty and common sense:

against the intuition and experience he had learned the hard way from tracking wild boar and tiger. But it was also a challenge to which something inside compelled him to respond, as if Woodford had thrown down the gauntlet and dared him to meet him, pistols at the ready, at dawn. What he was about to do would prove without doubt to Elizabeth that he, and not Woodford, was the worthier of her love.

As the preparations and excitement intensified, Carew saw less and less of Elizabeth who, with her usual enthusiasm, had flung herself headlong into the fray.

'There is simply so much to do,' she told him when he waylaid her a few days before the ball, as she hurried towards her father's bungalow. She was followed by two Indian myahs, carefully carrying a long muslin-wrapped object.

'It's my ball-gown,' Elizabeth told him excitedly. 'An exact copy of a model from a magazine I found in the Residency, as ancient as Kathmandu,' she laughed. 'That is all I can reveal. You will simply have to wait and see. But I think you will like it.'

'I like you as you are.'

Carew took her arm and drew her into the shadows of the small wooden chapel.

'I don't know, Elizabeth, if you realise what I really think about you.'

'A spoiled girl, headstrong and giddy, at least that's what the nuns used to say, and I'm sure I have not changed one bit since.'

Carew shook his head. 'What I see is a beautiful young woman, whose love I would do anything to win.'

A look of tenderness replaced the habitual playfulness of her blue eyes as she noted his serious demeanour.

'Oh, Tom, you know how hopelessly fond I am of you. I don't know what I would have done without you these past months. Everything here was so strange, so different, so frightening, and you made it all so bearable.'

'I want to mean everything to you, Elizabeth, like you mean to me.'

She tried to speak but he placed a finger on her lips.

'Don't say anything until I have proven the depth of my love. Just promise to meet me here at dawn on the morning of your birthday.'

'But what ...'

'Just promise ...'

She nodded, her eyes lighting up with excitement. 'You make it sound so mysterious, I cannot wait.'

He bent his head and kissed her gently on the check.

On the night before the ball Carew sat apart from his fellow officers in the mess-room. The conversation, the chink of glasses and the soft whine of the *punkahs*, as they displaced the hot air in feeble, barely discernible draughts, offering little relief to the company below, all seemed to be taking place at a distance from him. He felt at a remove from everything and everyone around him. In a trance-like state he sipped a whiskey and soda without tasting it. He did not feel the oppressive heat, the choking atmosphere of the smoke-filled mess, the drink-induced, loud laughter and talk of his companions, as they speculated about the forthcoming ball. He had dissolved into some strange world of his own.

'Hey, Carew, what are you giving her as a birthday present?'

'Better not ask, if you know what's good for you,' his companion cautioned him, with a wary eye towards the captain, slumped morosely in a chair near the window.

One of the subalterns strolled over in his direction.

'Are you all right, old man? You seem a bit down in the dumps. Come and join us for a rubber or two.'

Two eyes that seemed lost in some dark abyss focussed on the subaltern with difficulty. Without replying, Carew threw back the contents of his glass, got to his feet and disappeared into the night outside.

His companions watched his departure in sympathetic silence.

'Things not going too smooth in the love department, I'd venture,' one of them said.

'What odds Carew's chances against his betters tomorrow night?' the subaltern asked.

'No contest.'

A low laugh emanated from the company.

The journey through the inky blackness of the night seemed endless. The sky had been sullenly dark all day. The clouds had never rifted and now intercepted the light of both the stars and the moon. Carew could see but a few feet in front of him. An oppressive heat and silence seemed to bear down from above, as the earth held its breath for the imminent arrival of the monsoon. Slowly and with some difficulty, Carew's horse picked its way instinctively along the narrow, craggy trail. Silently he prayed that he would make it back to the cantonment before the monsoon broke and the trail became impassable. As he reached the outskirts of the village, a dog barked in the distance.

The dawn broke but was barely discernible from the night. The clouds roiled ever tighter and seemed to touch the ground. There was no let-up in the clammy, moisture-laden heat.

In the shadows, Elizabeth could feel the perspiration begin to soak through her morning dress as, with growing impatience, she waited for Carew. What on earth could be keeping him? If he did not come in another five minutes she vowed to return to her father's bungalow. Silently she upbraided herself for agreeing to meet with him on the morning of the most important day of her life, with so much left to do. Why could he not have given her his present at the ball, like Jeremy? It could not be that special. From what she had seen there was little to catch the eye in the tatty stores in Kathmandu. What could he possibly afford on his army pay, in any case, that could be so special?

Elizabeth had a delicious feeling that Jeremy's present, on the other hand, was going to turn out to be something really exciting. She was as certain as she could be that he was going to propose to her. He had dropped enough hints about emerald rings and life on his family estate in Hampshire. If he did, then she was resolved to accept. She could not expect to spend all her life with her father, going from one army post to the other, depending on officers like Tom Carew to while away the long hours of inactivity and boredom. She glanced skywards and sent a silent prayer to whatever god chose to hear that the rains would stay away until after the ball.

She heard a sound behind her and a shadowy figure emerged from the gloom.

'My God, what happened to you?'

Carew walked unsteadily towards her. An ugly red gash lay open across his forehead. His tunic was ripped and torn. His eyes were sunk in his head and he stared at her with an inhuman look out of his ashen face. He was like an apparition from the grave.

'I had a bit of an accident.' His voice sounded hoarse. 'But it was worth it.'

His hand fumbled inside the remnants of his tunic. He held something towards her. Elizabeth backed away in horror. In the palm of his hand an emerald eye looked up at her. She shook her head in disbelief.

'Yes, Elizabeth, for you. The green eye of the Yellow God, the gift you asked for, which Woodford had not the guts to get. Now you see which one of us deserves you.'

'Tom, have you lost your senses? You could be court-martialled for this.'

'You are worth the risk.'

'Are you mad? I only said it in jest. Look, Tom, I think you may have misunderstood, not just this, but a lot of things. Our friendship, you and I, is just that. It can never be anything more.'

'Why not?'

'Because ...' Elizabeth struggled to find the right words. 'Because, although I am very fond of you, I ... I'm afraid I don't love you. I'm sorry, Tom, but there it is.'

Carew looked at her uncomprehendingly.

'I really do think you should take it back,' she gestured to the emerald, 'before anyone discovers it is missing. Look, I have to fly. I'll see you at the ball.'

'It's Woodford. It has been all along.'

She looked at him. His eyes seemed so strangely empty of all light and emotion that for a moment she thought she was looking into the empty sockets of a skull. She shivered.

'Look here, Tom, I really must go. There is still an awful lot to do.'

She backed away from him before turning and hurrying towards her father's bungalow.

Behind her Carew lowered his eyes to the emerald in his hand, which he had chanced his life to get. He felt his life-blood suddenly drain from him.

The rain almost held off for Elizabeth's birthday ball. The Residency was decked out beyond her expectations. Everyone who had been invited had made the journey. The musicians from the army band played as well as if they were the band from the Savoy Hotel in London.

As she had anticipated, Jeremy proposed to her after they had finished their third dance. They had gone out onto the balcony to take what little air there was. A grumble of thunder echoing across the valley below did not intrude on his proposal of marriage, nor Elizabeth's accepting and allowing him to place the emerald ring on her finger. He kissed her passionately.

'Come, let's make the announcement.'

As another thunderclap rumbled towards them, Elizabeth put a restraining hand on his arm.

'Wait a while, there is something I must do first.'

Woodford frowned.

'Don't worry, it will only take a minute or two. I'll be back before you know I've gone,' Elizabeth said gaily as she hurried away.

She had not seen Tom Carew all evening. She feared that he was taking her rejection badly. Or maybe he had taken her advice and had returned to the village with the emerald eye. She sincerely hoped he had. As she crossed the barrack square, the dreamy air of a waltz tune came stealing softly through the gloom. She felt curiously light-headed with happiness.

As she approached Carew's room, a flash of blue-white lightning lit up the murky sky and revealed the door of his room, which was open wide. Another thunderclap, this time nearer, rent the air.

'Tom, are you there?'

There was no reply. Cautiously she entered his room. The ground beneath her feet seemed strangely slippery. She could see his outline, lying flat on his back on the narrow army cot. There was something unnerving about the all-too-still shape.

'Tom,' she whispered.

As if in answer, another flash of lightning lit up the interior and revealed to her eyes the ugly dagger that lay buried to the hilt in his heart.

Elizabeth screamed and ran out into the night as the skies opened and the rain fell in torrents onto the parched earth.

Ghost Story

THE MINUTE she set eyes on Joe's wife, Sheila knew that it was going to be a tough two weeks ahead. There was that look of 'I don't want to be here and you're going to know about it' in the American woman's aloof demeanour and in her disdainful glance when Joe first introduced them at Dublin Airport.

'This is my wife, Ruby,' her bother-in-law said, as he drew the petite, composed, unsmiling woman into the excited and emotional reunion that was taking place in Arrivals between him and his younger brother, Rose's husband, Tim.

Shyly and awkwardly the two brothers had embraced, bridging a forty-year span of separation and alienation in two instinctive and emotion-filled seconds. Sheila felt the tears prick at her eyelids and stood back, not willing to intrude on their moment.

For those few seconds Ruby had been ignored and it was obvious that she was not accustomed to being sidelined. Sheila turned towards her, arms outstretched to embrace her brother-in-law's wife. But the look that emanated from those granite, blue-grey eyes made Sheila stop short and merely touch the reluctantly extended hand.

'You're very welcome. We have been looking forward so much to meeting you.'

A smile briefly touched the American woman's face as her eyes flicked up and down. In that single glance Sheila got the feeling that everything about her, from her head to her heels, had been somehow registered, as if by some electronic device hidden behind the expressionless, unnaturally sleek face of her sister-in-law. It was, she thought, as if she had been examined by a metal detector: her appearance, her clothes scrutinised and calculated in one expert glance. Then, as Joe introduced his wife to his brother, Sheila did her own calculation.

The carefully made-up, unwrinkled visage of her sister-in-law defied nature, she reckoned, as much as it complimented the skill of the plastic surgeon. All traces of the passage of years, as well as all natural expression, had been obliterated from the smooth veneer. It was impossible to detect a single emotion in the American woman's face other than the look of perpetual surprise that the surgeon's knife had left behind. There was no loud American *bas-couture* on view in Ruby's dress. A classically tailored Chanel suit of shell-pink bouclé, knee-length, set off her model-shaped figure, slim legs and complimented her carefully arranged ash-blonde hair. A Gucci handbag (the real thing, Sheila noted) and a single row of pearls around her neck gave the impression of restrained elegance. Ruby was a glowing example of the best of American genetic modification and dress, which left her in some kind of an age limbo: anywhere between fifty and sixty, Sheila reckoned. A steel magnolia, she concluded and wondered how on earth Ruby and Joe had got together.

She looked across at the genial face of her brother-in-law whose arm was still around her husband. Unlike his wife, Joe had done little to conceal his years. His balding head, florid face and ample paunch made him look every bit his sixty years. Yet in comparison to his wife, there was something reassuringly natural about him.

'Well, how about it? Can you believe this, honey? Me and my little brother together after all this time.'

Ruby ignored Joe and turned to Sheila.

'This farm of yours, how long will it take to get there?'

'Two, two and a half hours, depending on the traffic.'

The hard eyes narrowed in annoyance.

'You can't be serious. Two, three hours on the road.' She

rounded on her husband. 'We have to over-night.'

Sheila exchanged a glance with her husband. She had been up half the night before preparing the dinner she had planned for their guests' arrival. She had spent days cleaning the house. Tim had spent a small fortune in having an en suite installed in the guest bedroom. The entire house had been painted, inside and out. The garden had been tidied, weeded and pruned into order. Even the farmyard and sheds had been given a major overhaul. Everything was in readiness. An overnight stay in Dublin, even if they could get accommodation at such short notice, would spoil weeks of planning and preparation. And Tim would have to make arrangements with a neighbour to see to the animals.

Joe saw their unease and disappointment. The only thing that mattered to him was to get to see the old place as soon as possible. But he had to be careful with Ruby or else, as experience had painfully taught him in the past, she would dig in her heels and refuse to budge. He put his arm around her and hugged her carefully.

'Ah, sugar, it will be a cakewalk, I promise. You can take the front seat. Have a nap on the way. We'll be there in no time and you can rest up all day tomorrow.'

'It might be difficult to get suitable accommodation at this short notice, Ruby,' Tim added.

'This is a city?'

'Well, yes,' Tim laughed, unperturbed by her sarcasm, 'but maybe we're not quite up to American speed yet. Anyway it would be great to get you and Joe home as soon as we can.'

'There's nothing I'd like more, kid.'

With ill-disguised displeasure Ruby shrugged her elegant shoulders. 'Well, I must eat. That garbage they served on the plane was revolting.'

Sheila thought of the veritable feast awaiting them at home. Tim caught her glance and shrugged.

Two hours later, when Ruby's appetite had been appeased at the airport restaurant, they set out westwards. Sheila, Tim and an embarrassed Joe had toyed with their salads and endured Ruby's litany of complaints about the food, which she barely touched. A marbling of fat on her sirloin of steak was greeted with disdain.

'Really, you people have no idea. Do you not care about your health over here?'

'It keeps the meat tender in the cooking,' Tim patiently explained.

'Fat equals fat in anybody's language,' Ruby replied as she pushed her plate aside.

'That must be why Americans top the obesity table.'

The words had left her lips before Sheila realised.

'She's gotcha there, babe.' Joe laughed.

The grey-blue eyes flicked balefully at Sheila.

'Not this American.'

Sheila could have kicked herself. She knew how much this reunion meant to Tim. He had planned and prepared for it for so long. She wanted everything to go as smoothly as possible. Silently she vowed to bite her tongue in future and let Ruby have her way for the duration of their stay, for Tim and Joe's sake.

Ruby opted for the back seat of the car and, with a black-out mask over her eyes and a travel pillow tucked behind her head, much to everyone's relief, promptly fell asleep.

'Holy mackerel, I can't believe how the old country has changed. Look at these roads. It's just like everywhere else.' Joe shook his head in disbelief.

'Hang on until we get over to the west – the roads there will make you'll feel more at home, believe me,' Tim laughed.

'Gee, Sheila, you cannot imagine what this trip means to me. Forty years. Over half a lifetime. I should never have left it so long.'

Sheila patted Joe's shoulder.

'Well, you're here now and that is all that matters. You'll catch up on everything in no time. We haven't changed that much you know.'

'Are the Sheridans still living?' Joe asked.

'Old Pat and Nora are gone,' Tim told him. 'But Johnny, he was in your class at school, remember, he runs the farm now. He's planning a night out for you with a few of the lads from your class.'

'And that will be some night, I can tell you, Joe. You'll need to be on your toes to survive Johnny Sheridan's definition of a "good night",' Sheila added.

'I bet.' Joe cleared his throat and shifted his bulk in the seat in front of her. 'I have to be careful with Ruby, you know. She doesn't quite understand all this going back, reminiscing and stuff.'

He turned and looked apprehensively back at the figure of his wife and continued in a whisper. 'If the truth be known, I had some job to get her to come in the first place. Don't want to push my luck, if you know what I mean?'

'How did you two meet?' Tim asked.

'My company put in some electric shutters in her apartment in Brooklyn. Bit of a problem with payment. I had to go over myself to sort it out. She had just got divorced and well … sorta took a fancy to me. Couldn't believe my luck. She could have had anybody. She was some looker, I can tell you.'

'And she still is, isn't she, Sheila?' Tim said.

Sheila looked sideways at the chic figure, age-defying profile and blonde hair and, in all honesty, had to agree.

'She certainly is, Joe. You have obviously looked after her well.'

'Well, Ruby sure knows how to give the ole credit card a good work-out,' he laughed. 'But, gee, I'm not complaining. She's worth it.'

It was late evening when they arrived at the farm. The ivy-clad farmhouse was bathed in the sunset's glow, its windows, upstairs and down, gleaming like beaten gold, warm and inviting. Transfixed, Joe stood and stared at the house of which he had dreamed and thought during years of bad times and good in America. He reached into his pocket, took out a handkerchief and blew his nose before turning away to conceal his emotion. Tim and Sheila pretended not to notice and carried the bags inside.

'Joe, I ache all over. Run me a bath.'

Ruby stepped into the hall and looked around her.

'Let me show you to your room, Ruby,' Sheila offered. 'The boys will bring the bags up.'

She led her guest upstairs and into the newly decorated guest room.

Ruby shivered and looked around. 'You do have central heating, I hope.'

Although it was late summer, the evening was still warm. Sheila smiled.

'Tim will see to it right away. Here is your bathroom. Do make yourself at home.'

'Well, isn't this cosy?' Joe commented as he followed Tim with the bags into the room. 'You guys have sure done great things with the old homestead. Real comfortable, not like I used to remember. Water from the well. The outside john. The turf fireplace. The brass paraffin lamp on the table. The –'

'Oh, for God's sake, Joe. Don't you know it's a dead giveaway of old age, talking about the past,' Ruby interrupted him.

'Any Irish connections, yourself, Ruby?' Sheila intervened.

Ruby shrugged. 'I'm not into that kind of thing. Live for today is my motto.'

'You two have a rest, a shower, whatever, and we'll see you downstairs later for dinner. Say about seven?'

'That'll do just fine, brother,' Joe said from the bathroom as he started to draw a bath for his wife.

Tim and Sheila closed the door on their guests.

'You expect me to put up with this for two whole weeks?'

Ruby's words seemed intended to be overheard by her hosts. Tim looked at Sheila and shook his head. She followed him downstairs.

'By God, that is some self-centred woman above. I'd say Joe has his hands well full with her,' Tim commented as he helped Sheila put the finishing touches to the table in the kitchen.

'Now maybe you'll appreciate me a bit more,' Sheila laughed. 'Or else I'll take to giving the ole credit card a good work-out too.'

Tim came over to the Aga and gave her a hug.

'Yeah, Ruby makes me appreciate just what I've got, right enough.'

'Well, they're only here for a fortnight. So for Joe's sake we'll have to put up with her.'

'If you can, I will,' Tim said. 'In view of what happened between him and the old man, I feel it's the least I can do. Anyway, brother or no, I like Joe. He's a good guy.'

'Why is it always the nice guys that get saddled with the Rubys of this world?'

Tim looked in mock hurt at his wife.

'Ah, you know what I mean.'

Tim smiled and nodded. 'One of life's unsolved mysteries. It looks great,' he said pointing to the table, dressed in a pale pink damask, best cutlery and china dinner service set for four.

Sheila placed a cut-glass bowl of sweet pea from the garden in the centre as a final touch.

'Maybe I should have served it after all in the dining-room, for the sake of her Ladyship.' She gestured towards the ceiling.

'You heard what Joe said on the way down. This is where he had his last meal with my mother, the day he went away. Never saw her again. She was broken-hearted. Joe was her favourite. Anyway it looks great, thanks love.'

'Well, it's not every day you find a brother after forty years.'

In the end it was just the three of them who sat down to dine.

'Ruby's fragile, you see,' Joe explained. 'Can't over-do things.'

'Oh, does she suffer from some illness?' Tim asked.

'Oh no. Fit as a fiddle. Just the travel, jet lag, new people, you know how it is.'

They nodded sympathetically.

'I guess Ruby is what you might call a Manhattan Miss, never happy away from the Big Apple. A born and bred New Yorker, not a Paddy like me.'

Sheila and Tim exchanged a glance. It was obvious that Joe was trying his best to cover for his wife's absence.

'She'll possibly feel fine tomorrow,' Sheila assured him. 'A good night's sleep will work wonders. Is there anything Ruby would like to do while she's here – sightseeing, shopping?'

'Well, whatever about seeing the sights, shopping is what she's best at. Maybe a trip to Galway.'

'No problem,' Tim said. 'We can see to that whenever she likes. Now how about you and I go walkabout and see what you think of the old place?'

Joe's face lit up with a broad smile. 'Thought you'd never ask. But before that can I tell you, Sheila, that I've never had anything like this, not for forty years. Meat you can taste, vegetables you can recognise and that apple pie was to die for. God knows what we're doing to our food in the States.'

'Go on with you,' Sheila smiled. 'It was just an old-fashioned Irish meal, no frills.'

'And all the better for that, you gotta believe it.'

The long twilight of the late summer's evening had begun to throw shadows across the yard as the brothers walked towards the gate leading out to the fields. The yard, stables and barns looked tidy and well kept: farm machinery and implements neatly stacked. The additional coat of whitewash on the out-buildings made everything look pristine, Tim was glad to see.

'God, I hardly recognise the old place.' Joe stopped and looked around. 'The old man never kept it like this. All muck and shit. But he was right in one thing, you'd make the better farmer.'

Tim shrugged. 'Who's to know? If things had been different, maybe you –'

'We won't go down that road,' Joe interrupted. 'What's done is done. It would never have worked out. I could see that. I was better away from him.'

'Well, he'd have been proud of you and how well you've done in America.'

They walked through the near field, already wet with dew, towards the small hill that formed the centre of the hundred-acre farm.

'I doubt it, kid. He would have got more satisfaction if I had to crawl back and ask him for help.' A bitter edge crept into Joe's voice. 'When I came home after putting in a fourteen-hour day, holding down two jobs, back to the flop-house I called home in Queen's, I swore to God that I'd hit Skid Row before I'd ever come back and ask him for anything.'

'Well, you at least stood up to him.'

'Yeah, and look where it got me.'

Tim stole a glance at his brother. 'But you like America. You're successful, married, happy, aren't you?'

Joe stopped as they reached the gently sloping summit of the hill. He was nearly out of breath from the exertion. He remembered when they were kids how they used to race each other to the top to see who could first spot the peak of Cruaghmore in the distance. From their vantage point he looked around him.

It was almost unchanged from the image he had carried with him into exile, deep inside, to be used like a salve when the loneliness got too much: cows grazing on green grass, swallows swooping, the sound of water tripping over the stones in the stream nearby. He loved it all with an emigrant's exaggeration and intensity and he felt somehow vindicated that it was still there after all this time. That was what brought him back, to check it out, to see if the mirage that had sustained him for forty years was real.

'If the truth were known, I guess I haven't been happy since the day I left. The row with the old man was the excuse I needed to convince myself that I had made the right move. I was fooling myself, just making my wrong choice bearable. I let things slide. Never thought I'd stay on so long. Until one day I woke up to the fact that I'd been in the States longer than here. Ruby, well, it was better than staring at the four walls, I suppose. No, kid, to be honest, its all been one big fucking waste of time, my time, and I sure as hell ain't got much of that left.'

Tim put his arm on Joe' shoulder. 'Look, we all make the wrong choices – some big, some not so big. You're here now. Back where you belong. Did you ever think of stopping, permanently, like? There's a site for a house here for you anytime. Sheila and I decided that a long time ago.'

Joe looked at his brother and shook his head in wonderment.

'You know, that's the first time anyone has offered me anything. Since the day I left I've always had to fend for myself. Anything I got, I got myself. I sure appreciate it, kid, more than you know.'

'Well? What do you say?'

Joe sighed. 'I'd jump at it, if it were just me. I'm ready to come back. Have been for a long while. Maybe it's to do with age but the bitterness and anger seem all eaten up now. But Ruby?' He shrugged. 'No Macy's, no Saks. Fashion shows and cocktails. Lunches with her girlfriends that run into dinner. Winter in Florida, we have a place there.' He smiled ruefully. 'No offence, but for Ruby it would be sheer torture.'

They retraced their steps through the fields.

'But hey, kid, right now is good enough for me and I sure aim to make this the best holiday ever,' Joe said and put his arm around his brother.

Sheila knew it would be difficult but not as bad as it turned out. From the first day of their holiday Ruby seemed intent on making it as unbearable for everyone as she could. She may have been on a farm in the west of Ireland but she made it plain that she would not be making any allowances in her expectations and demands. From the outset she set out her marker as to what she would do and not do. Nothing outside the house interested her and, despite Joe's coaxing, she refused to leave the sitting-room, where she spent most of the day resting and reading the pile of magazines she had brought with her.

'If looking at cows in a field makes you happy, don't expect me to get excited.'

She seemed totally self-obsessed and had absolutely no concern or conception of anyone else's needs, particularly those of her husband. Like some sleek spider, she seemed to have Joe entrapped in a web that kept him scurrying around her in circles in an unending but futile quest to please her.

On the very first morning Sheila had set the table for breakfast in the dining-room, she had decided, in the expectation that Ruby would join them. As she dressed the table with her best china from the cabinet, sounds emanated from the kitchen. She looked at her watch. It was just past eight. Tim had gone out to tend to the cattle earlier and she presumed that their guests were still sound asleep.

'Oh, good morning, Joe. I thought you'd be still sleeping off the jet lag.'

'So did I, but Ruby is wide awake and wants her breakfast.'

'Why did she not just come down? I have everything ready. Full Irish or, if she'd prefer, something lighter.'

'Well, I usually get her fixed up before I go to work at home. I guess old habits die hard. Anyway, I have to get her supplements ready.' He held up a self-seal plastic bag filled with individual packets. 'Can't take them in pill form, don't agree with her. Gotta be made up from powder. Guess I could qualify as a chemist at this stage.'

Sheila looked on as Joe measured various potions into three small glasses. She noticed that his face looked tired and drawn.

'You could do with some supplements and rest yourself, Joe. Here, let me make you a nice cup of tea.'

'I'd better see to Ruby first.'

Sheila nodded and smiled sympathetically. Better not interfere, she thought. Joe would undoubtedly come out the worst of it.

As it was, judging by the sound of Ruby's tones from above, he was already in the wars and was back down the stairs almost immediately.

'She's left one of her supplements at home. Is there a health food outlet anywhere nearby? You know, one that sells this kinda stuff.'

'Well, not in the village, Joe. Maybe in town the chemist might stock something like that. The nearest health-food stores are in Galway, I'm afraid.'

'Could you possibly give me a lift into town? She gets a bit panicky without the stuff.'

Sheila looked at her watch. 'Chemist won't open for another two hours. Look, I'll make some fresh orange juice. That might tide her over.'

Joe looked doubtful. 'Thanks, Sheila. I guess we're a load of trouble and we ain't even started our holiday.'

Tim drove him later into the town. The chemist did not stock the supplement and directed them to a health-food shop in Galway. It was late afternoon before they returned. Ruby was reading a copy of *Harpers and Queen* in the sitting-room.

'Where were you? I've been stuck here all day with nothing to do.'

Even Joe shook his head in disbelief.

'Haring over the country for this.' He handed her the supplement.

'Oh, that. I found my own a while ago. Packed it in another bag.' Ruby shrugged.

Joe slumped into the couch. 'Well, I guess, Tim, that's women for you.'

Some women, Tim thought to himself. 'What about a drink, Joe? I think we've earned it.'

'Joe doesn't drink in the middle of the day,' Ruby intervened.

'Well, honey, on this occasion, I think I'll make an exception.'

Tim felt like clapping his brother on the back. Ruby gave her husband a look that could kill at forty paces and resumed her reading.

But Joe's act of defiance did not go unpunished and Ruby's revenge extended to include Tim and Sheila. Anything they planned, like dinner at a nearby lakeside restaurant, trips to town, visits to the neighbours, even the shopping trip to Galway, had to be abandoned, usually at the last moment, on Ruby's account.

'How can any human being be so regularly afflicted with fatigue, migraine, upset stomachs and other ailments I've never even heard of and still look so healthy?' Tim asked Sheila.

'It's a gift,' Sheila assured him. 'And Ruby sure has it.'

'By God, she is one selfish woman. She's ruining Joe's holiday, not to mention driving me around the bend. It's as if she cannot abide to see him enjoy himself. How in God's name did he fall for someone like that after being a bachelor for so long?'

'Maybe there's your answer,' Sheila said. 'On his own for too long. In panic falls for the wrong woman. It happens. We'll just have to put up with her, for Joe's sake. There's only another week to go.'

In the event, the situation reached crisis point sooner than they imagined. Johnny Sheridan's proposed night out for the boys brought it to a head.

'If you expect me to sit here waiting for you to fall into bed after a night's boozing, you've got another thought coming. I'm telling you, Joe, I'm out of here.'

'One night to meet up with the boys, that's all I'm asking.'

'You know how drink upsets me. Anyway, I've had enough of this trip-down-memory-lane stuff. I'm going home.'

'We can't just walk out like that. There's another week to go.'

Ruby shrugged her elegant shoulders. 'Maybe you can't but I can,' she said coldly as she opened the wardrobe and started to take out her clothes. 'I knew it was a mistake from the start. I didn't want to come but of course you insisted. Well, you can't say I didn't try. I've put in my time in this backwoods but enough is enough.'

'What am I supposed to say to Tim and Sheila? They have done everything humanly possible to make you feel at home.'

Ruby gave him a look of indifference. 'Tell them what you like.'

'Look, Joe, you don't need to apologise to us,' Sheila said when Joe told them. 'We can see that Ruby is not happy here. Ireland is not everyone's cup of tea, much as we like to think otherwise.'

'I feel so … embarrassed, ungrateful. After all you've done.'

'There's no need to feel either embarrassed or ungrateful. At least you and Tim met up again after all these years.'

'Can't you stay on and let Ruby go back on her own?' Tim asked.

'Tim,' Sheila admonished.

'She's a grown woman, for God's sake. If she's so intent on getting home, surely she's capable of going on her own steam.'

'Couldn't do that, kid. Ruby absolutely dreads flying.'

'Well, all I can say is, you've the patience of Job.'

'Comes with the territory, kiddo.' Joe shrugged.

Sheila flashed Tim a look to say nothing more. It was obvious that Joe was embarrassed and crestfallen enough.

'Look, all I can say is sorry. And I promise you both that, if you'll invite me, I'll come back next year, but this time on my own.'

'You'll always be welcome, Joe, whenever you decide.'

Tim nodded in agreement. 'Anytime.'

'Then that makes the parting easier.'

At the airport, looking as chic and aloof as the day they first met, Ruby extended her hand to Sheila.

'Well, perhaps we may see you stateside sometime.'

The invitation was issued in tones that brooked no possibility of it ever being accepted.

'I doubt it,' Sheila said. 'Europe is more to our liking.'

The cold eyes registered Sheila's intended slight and the elegant shoulders raised in a shrug. With the merest wave of her hand to Tim, Ruby made for the entrance to the departure gates, as if she could not wait to get away.

'Well, what can I say, only sorry things turned out this way and that you guys are something special.' Joe looked away. 'And now that we kinda found each other, I sure don't want to lose you all over again. Hope this … hitch won't change that.'

'Listen here, Joe, no matter what, Sheila and I won't let that happen.'

'You'll come back next year and we won't take no for an answer,' Sheila added.

'Joe,' Ruby called impatiently from the departure entrance.

Joe kissed Sheila and hugged his brother. There were tears in his eyes as he picked up Ruby's vanity case.

'So help me God, as sure as I am holding this, I promise you that this day, this time, next year I will be back in the old home. And I won't bring Ruby.'

Sheila and Tim watched Joe disappear.

'Do you think he means it?' Sheila asked.

'He means it all right. Whether he's allowed to do it is another thing. Come on, love, let's go home.'

From the kitchen window, Sheila stopped peeling the potatoes to watch the last rays of the sunset slowly sink below the outline of the hill. She wiped her forehead with the back of her hand. Late evening though it was, the temperature had scarcely dropped from midday. The very air was heat-laden and so still that she was conscious of every tick of the wag-on-the-wall cloak. She wondered how Tim had got on at the mart. She looked at the clock. Half past eight. His lot would only be going up now and, between the paperwork and the journey home, she did not expect him for another two hours or so.

She felt a stream of perspiration trickle down her back. It was unnaturally hot for this late in the evening, like the heat before a thunderstorm, she thought. She looked out the window. The evening sky was cloudless with no indication of any such possibility. Beside her, Ben, their sheepdog, whined and stood up sniffing the air.

A loud thud at the front door made her jump. It didn't sound like someone knocking, rather as if something had been dumped down on the step outside. She wiped her hands on a towel and pushed back the damp tentacles of hair from her forehead. She went to the door and opened it but there was no one there. She stepped outside and looked down the short driveway. Not a soul.

You're imagining things, she scolded herself.

As she closed the front door, a loud rapping sound of

someone knocking on a window made her hurry into the sit-ting-room from where she thought the sound had come. She looked out through both windows in the room but could see nothing. The rapping sound now seemed to come from the kitchen. Maybe somebody had gone around the back while she had gone to answer the front door? She hurried into the kitchen. Again nothing. Suddenly she felt a tingle of fear as she saw Ben rise from where he was lying and slowly back away from the door, the hair around his neck standing upright. A low, almost unnatural, growl reverberated deep in his throat. She rushed to the back door and turned the lock.

Burglars, she thought and ran to the phone. Just then the rapping sound started up again, this time on all the downstairs windows simultaneously. My God, there must be a few of them, she thought desperately, her fingers shaking as she punched out the numbers of Tim's mobile. The racket was growing more intense and seemed to make the whole house shake. Ben was howling like a hound. She listened as Tim's answer service informed her that he had it switched off. She slammed down the receiver and dialled 999.

'I tell you, there was someone trying to get into the house. I'm not imagining it, Tim. I know what I heard.'

'Well, whoever it was, they're well gone now. The Guards have checked the whole place over and found no sign of an attempted break in. Maybe it was some of the village kids, kicking ball or fooling around.'

Sheila shook her head. 'It wasn't kids, of that I'm certain. I suppose we'll never know who it was.'

By the time Ruby got around to writing to them, Joe was dead and buried almost a month.

'My only brother. Not to know that he died. God, I could strangle that woman gladly. I should have been there, brought his body home to be buried here, not among strangers.' Tim threw Ruby's card with its brief message from him in disgust.

Sheila squeezed his hand in sympathy. 'Never mind, love. Joe knew how much you cared. Just be thankful that you both got a chance to meet up again. That week last year was worth all of Ruby's tantrums. You know how much it meant to Joe.'

'A year, my God it only seems like last week. Little did I think I'd never see him again. And he was so looking forward to coming back. Never got the chance.'

Sheila picked up Ruby's card. 'When exactly did he die? The twenty-ninth of August,' she read. 'That was mart day wasn't it?'

She ran to the Co-op calendar hanging at the side of the food press. Tom always encircled mart days in red. She thumbed through the pages. 'Yes, the twenty-ninth of August.' She turned to Tim. 'The same day I thought we were being burgled.'

Sheila thought back to that day and the urgent, unrelenting knocking on the windows and doors and smiled.

'Maybe Joe did come back, as he promised, after all.'

Finding Tom Cruise

THE FACE, handsome, if serious, had looked out at me for as long as I could remember from its black frame on the mahogany sideboard in the sitting-room. Because of its sepia colour, it appeared different to the rest of my mother's ever-expanding collection of family photographs, which stood to attention on the highly polished surface.

As teenagers we had cringed to see ourselves thus displayed at various stages of growth: in momentary angelic poses in communion dresses; in outdated kilts and cotton dresses; with pigtails, ponytails, tousled and curly hairstyles and gap-toothed smiles. Behind our mother's back we often sought to consign some of the most unflattering exhibits to the drawers underneath, only later to find them rescued and put back on display by their vigilant keeper. His photograph, however, remained unmoved from where it always stood on the top left-hand corner.

Often as a child I was made dust the entire collection, usually as a punishment for some misdemeanour or other. His photo, I recall, always seemed to dissipate my anger and make me apply the dust cloth more gently to the glass. The steady, somewhat serious eyes looked directly up at me, unsmiling from under the peak of an army cap. His complexion was fair, his features fine but purposeful. Solid shoulders were enhanced by the epaulettes of a jacket adorned with military insignia. Despite the trace of sadness that I imagined I detected around his eyes, he seemed an altogether sort of man, someone who knew what he was about. He seemed old to me then, like someone from a distant era.

'That's your Uncle Tom, my oldest brother,' my mother had told me. 'He died in the war.'

'What war?'

'World War Two.'

'But Ireland was not in the war.' That much I knew, despite the fact that the history I learned at school stopped short at 1916.

'He was in the American Air Force.'

'How did he die?'

My mother took the picture from me and gazed at the likeness of her brother for a moment before gently placing the frame back in its allotted place on the sideboard.

'He was killed in a plane crash, poor thing.'

And that was all I had ever known about my long-dead uncle Tom Cruise and it was enough to satisfy the surface curiosity of my youth.

It was many years later when, as an adult, my uncle re-entered my life and my quest to find out more about him started.

About to embark on a holiday to Florida, I spoke of my plans.

'That's where your Uncle Tom died,' my mother said.

'I thought he died in the war.'

'He was only being trained.'

'Where in Florida?'

'I'm not sure. He wrote to me once from somewhere there.'

After a rummage through a box crammed with decades of letters, invoices and receipts, my mother eventually located his letter.

The letter was dated December 1942 and bore no address.

'Army regulations, I believe,' my mother said.

The handwriting was as steady and clear as the expression from the eyes that had looked out at me from the photograph. His style of writing was surprisingly fresh, articulate and so descriptive of Florida that it whetted my appetite for the holiday ahead.

> Well here I am in sunny Florida. The climate is ideal. Not surprisingly this is the winter vacation land for America. You should see the miles of beautiful beaches and palm trees, not to mention the thousands of acres of orange and grapefruit trees. It is beautiful.
>
> The people go out of their way to be friendly to us. Lots of times we are invited to their homes for dinner. I consider myself very fortunate to be stationed in such a wonderful place.

'Wasn't he just. It sounds more like a holiday than a war. I wonder why he was he there in the first place? Florida seems a long way from the battlefields of Europe.'

My mother shrugged. 'I knew so little about him and his life in the States. I barely remember him. He left for America when I was still very young.'

'To join the army?'

'No. He went to stay with an uncle, a brother of my father, in Massachusetts. Tom was very bright at school, I remember, and he had done very well for himself in America. He had become manager of a chain of stores, forerunners of the supermarkets. Enjoyed a good lifestyle. This is a photo he sent me from there when he was in civilian life.'

The tiny sepia photo showed a young man, fair-haired, confident and smiling, dressed in plus fours, a golf bag slung over his shoulder, his foot on the running board of a typical American-made car of the period.

'Yes, he had made a good life for himself in America,' my mother said. 'Then out of the blue, he just left it all behind to join the army. Volunteered, in fact. I remember my parents being so shocked and worried.'

'Well, I'm not surprised he volunteered. I doubt my holiday will be as good. Listen to this.'

> Our life in the service is not all work. Some weekends we really have a wonderful time. For instance we take in a football game, have dinner and a few cocktails, see a show or go dancing with some Southern Belles!

'He sounds quite a swinger.'

My mother smiled. 'Well, at least he enjoyed himself while he could. He was dead three months after he wrote that letter. And all his life ahead of him.'

'Maybe he joined because of girlfriend trouble?'

> I am still very much single. I came close to getting hitched, some time back. But when she started to dictate my way of living, that was enough. I got free very quickly. We still are friends but that is all.

Her mother nodded at the words. 'Even when we were children, Tom always seemed to know his own mind. No one could push him around. Self-contained, I think you'd call it today.'

'He sounds so ... with it, so modern.'

'Well, he was only thirty-two, you know. Not exactly ancient.' My mother looked quizzically at me.

'I know,' I nodded, suddenly remembering that I was ten years older than he had been when he had written the letter.

I glanced at my uncle's photograph in its usual slot on the sideboard nearby. The eyes looked back at me with their steady intensity. Among the collection his photograph always imbued an air of mystery or maybe aloofness, of being somehow different from the rest. The photographs of family, relations and friends encapsulated uncomplicated moments in the minutiae of ordinary domestic life. His photo stood out, evocative as it was of something foreign and vaguely frightening: of a war that, while fought all but on our very doorstep, seemed as remote and irrelevant to my generation as it had in reality been to my parents who had lived through it. Yet somewhere in the Sunshine State of America, out of reach of bomb and bullet, out of sight of Europe's agony, to a young man from Mayo this far-away war had somehow become so relevant that it had both changed and ended his life.

I looked again at his photo. Was there also a look of censure in his eyes? I was of a generation born after the war that knew or cared little about it. It was no more relevant to me than any other war in history. If anything, I knew more about the Hundred Years War or the Napoleonic Wars than I did about Dunkirk or Pearl Harbor, milestones in a conflict that would ever remain alien to the Irish psyche. And yet my uncle had somehow died, if not in it, then because of it. Maybe, through him, I could learn more and perhaps understand what made him become part of it.

'Pity we don't know more about him – why he joined up, how he ended up in Florida, where he was stationed.' I looked at my mother. 'What really happened to him?'

'Well, he wrote more to my mother. Perhaps the letters are still at home.'

On the way back to Dublin, I stopped at my uncle's birthplace, where his younger brother still lived.

'Here you are,' my uncle said extending an old biscuit box. 'You'll find whatever he wrote in here.'

'Do you remember him?'

'Vaguely. I was only four when he left for America. But I clearly remember the day. Father and Mother were broken-hearted. It was as if they knew they would never see him again. And they never did. They could not understand why he volunteered, especially when he was doing so well for himself in civilian life. It took them a long time to get over his death.'

In Dublin I took out my uncle's letters one by one. They covered just over a year, from the date Tom Cruise had joined the American Air Force in January 1942 to the month of his death in March 1943. I spread the letters out on the table. A year in the life of Tom Cruise. It was strange, I thought, as I put them into chronological order, that only the letters he had written to his mother during the brief period of his army service had survived the intervening fifty years since his death. Letters he may have written to her from America prior to him joining the forces had somehow vanished.

First I was determined to know what had made him abandon his career, which he obviously enjoyed and at which he had been successful, to volunteer and join up. From his first letter home, dated 10 March 1942, I saw that he had joined the American Forces on 13 January 1942.

> I did not have to join but I felt it was my duty to do so. Of course it changes your whole life but I wanted to do my part.

In view of such patriotic sentiments, girlfriend trouble now seemed an almost frivolous reason. But my uncle was Irish, I thought; Ireland, not America, was his country. A cursory glance, however, through his letters revealed that before he had joined up he had, in fact, become an American citizen. Furthermore, from both the language and sentiments expressed in his letters, it became apparent that over the decade he had lived in America, Tom Cruise had become as Americanised as cherry pie and soda fountains. He had embraced the American way and in turn it had embraced him. America had made him and it was America, not Ireland, which had become the recipient of his loyalty.

> America is a wonderful country. It will always be a great country. There is no force in the world to stop us when we get rolling ... Please God before long we will have the enemy completely licked.

The words and sentiments could have been written by any all-American boy from Minnesota to Mississippi, rather than by a young man from County Mayo.

A check of pivotal dates in the war provided a possible reason for the actual timing of his enlistment. On 7 December 1941, Japan had attacked Pearl Harbor and America had entered the war. It was a time of great patriotic fervour. Before that event the war had been somewhere 'over there', distant and removed from American everyday life. But the unprovoked attack on the American base at Pearl Harbor changed all that.

Less than a month later, Tom Cruise was a corporal in the Air Corps. He had enlisted with a friend in St Louis and almost immediately had been sent for training to Florida. It became evident also from his letters that the Air Force was his preferred choice and to become a bomber pilot his dream. But even at this early stage he had encountered an obstacle in fulfilling that part of his ambition and wrote to his parents of his disappointment.

> The fellow I joined the army with is gone to Flying Cadet School. We were great friends. I gave him his first job in the store. How I wish I could go flying too but the age limit is twenty-seven. [He was then thirty-two]

Despite the setback, however, Tom Cruise never abandoned his desire to fly and bided his time to seize his chance.

All his letters were written from various Air Force bases in Florida but, like a well-trained soldier, he gave few clues as to the nature of his military duties in the service. Except for one, written from the air base in Jacksonville, none bore the name of his actual location. In one of his letters he advises his mother to send her letters to him care of a friend in Massachusetts who would know where he was based at any given time.

A few letters, I noticed, bore the legend *Idle Gossip Sinks Ships*, printed in bold lettering at the end of the page.

What ships, I wondered, and why should anonymity and guarded words be a military requirement in safe and sunny

Florida, far from the amphitheatre of the war? And why had my uncle been stationed in Florida of all places? From his letter to my mother it sounded as if Florida in the 1940s was every bit the sunshine playground that my holiday brochures of the 1990s promised.

The reasons for the secrecy and the cautionary legend displayed on my uncle's letters, as well as the enviable location of his posting, became evident when I started to research Florida's World War Two experience. Despite its location (or, as I found out, because of it) the caution displayed in my uncle's letters was surprisingly well warranted.

One month after Tom Cruise had joined the service and a few days after his arrival for training in Florida, a German U-boat had sunk the *Pan Massachusetts* south of Cape Canaveral. Five days later the *Republic* met a similar fate off West Palm Beach and in May the *Portero del Llano* was attacked by a German submarine within sight of Miami Beach. A few miles from where he was stationed in Jacksonville, German soldiers, who had come ashore from a submarine, were captured as they tried to blow up the railroad to prevent the shipment of war supplies from Florida. I found many other reports of German spying activity on military installations along the coast. Secrecy had thus become an essential weapon in the war effort in Florida, as much as in Europe, and this extended to the letters home of the servicemen in training camps there. Blackout regulations had also been introduced along Florida's long and exposed coastline, where lights from houses, hotels and amusement parks could silhouette allied merchant ships, making them sitting targets for the German U-boats that prowled the seas off the coastline.

Why Florida, this exotic outpost state, should have become the training hub for a war being fought faraway in Europe and in the Pacific eventually became evident. In the Roaring Twenties, Florida, with its superb climate and unspoiled landscape, had initially become America's winter playground. To indulge American desire for luxury and sun-shine all year round, new holiday complexes, even entire towns, such as the famous Coral Gables, had been developed to attract the wealthy down from the great cities up north. Every conceivable facility guaranteed those with the money the time of their lives in Florida's fancy hotels, speakeasies, racing tracks, casinos, theatres, restaurants and golden beach-es. The Great Depression of the 1930s, however, almost killed off Florida's fledging tourist industry and by 1940 the state had reverted back to being a sleepy, if sun-kissed, backwater. World War Two was destined to put the economy of Florida back into overdrive.

Florida's strategic location, with its long coastline facing the Atlantic, made it the vital first-line of defence, not merely for the southern United States, but also for the Caribbean and the Panama Canal. Even before America entered the war, when Tom Cruise was still managing his store in Massachusetts, there had been an upsurge in developing Florida's few military installations, including his first training post at Jackonsville Naval Air Station, one of its largest.

> I am with the Observation Squadron. At the moment my duties are mainly clerical. All the fellows in the squadron are swell.
>
> They are from every State … I am the only one from Ireland and when my friends found out they have been asking me all sorts of questions about the place. If we ever get shipped over there I sure will have a lot of questions to answer!

After Pearl Harbor and the entry of America into the war that had been raging in Europe for the previous two years, Florida became transformed. From just eight military installations in 1940, by 1943 one hundred and seventy-two had been established throughout the State. Military schools were built by the dozen to train recruits and soldiers from all over the United States and from other countries, such as Britain, Europe and South America as well. By the mid-1940s there were forty airfields alone in use within the state; Florida's flat terrain, clear skies and exceptional climate made it perfect for aviation training.

Hundreds of thousands of servicemen and women replaced the civilian tourists of the 1920s and early 1930s. The empty hotel rooms in the luxurious tourist hotels and complexes became barracks (the Federal Government paid the owners $20 per man/woman per month); the glitzy restaurants became mess halls; theatres became classrooms; and the golden beaches and the palm-dotted golf courses became military training fields and assault courses.

Tom Cruise was just one of over 600,000 service men who were trained in southern Florida during the war. The population was further enlarged by thousands of civilians who migrated into the state to work in the military installations, the steel and shipbuilding industries that had also become established there to service the war effort. From combat soldiers to bomber pilots, radio operators to sonar sound technicians, Florida (particularly southern Florida) was where the majority of American servicemen trained before being sent overseas for active service.

Life for these hundreds of thousands of recruits in the training camps in Florida was obviously more than bearable by army standards. From my uncle's letters (which because of the secrecy restrictions tended to concentrate on the personal side of his army life) it was evident that Florida was a choice posting and the conditions were not unduly onerous, as he wrote jocosely, if somewhat prophetically, home in September 1942.

> The regular hours, the exercise and plenty of sleep I'm getting will add ten years to my life!

When confined to camp, outside work hours, he relaxed with his comrades by playing ball, reading and watching movies. When on furlough, despite the restrictions and petrol shortages, he managed to travel extensively around the state.

I have several weekends off and see various new cities, although most of my travels have been confined to the South.

It was while posted at the Air Base in Jacksonville in September 1942 that Tom answered his mother's query regarding army diet.

> You asked about the food, Mother, well since we have been down here it is very good. Sunday for instance he had turkey and all the fixings, including strawberry shortcake, for dinner.

Not bad fare by any standards and it must have been reassuring to an Irish mother (and one whom, I recall, presided over one of the most hospitable of houses) to know that her boy was being well catered for in the culinary department! The climate also, particularly from autumn to early summer, was an added bonus to soldiering in Florida, as Tom indicated in a letter in November 1942.

> The weather here in Florida is ideal. It is called the Sunshine State and it certainly lives up to its name.

The facilities, both natural and man-made, the unspoiled and uncrowded environment, as well as the weather, induced many of the soldiers, sailors, airmen and marines who had trained there to take up permanent residence in the Sunshine State after the war, adding to the post-war boom Florida subsequently experienced.

Furloughs provided an outlet for the soldiers to let their hair down or, in Tom's case, to have it cut!

> I left camp early this morning. Since then I had a haircut, a shoeshine, did some shopping and had dinner. I also took in a movie, a good one, Eagle Squadron, about the adventures of some of the American boys fighting with the RAF.

The list of activities and entertainment that he participated in was testimony that army life in Florida was, as he wrote, not too bad at all. While, like the rest of America, Florida experienced war-time shortages, rationing, driving restrictions, even blackouts, the tourist infrastructure, for which Florida had become famous in the 1920s, now proved a welcome boon to the serviceman's life there.

The most famous hot spot was undoubtedly Miami Beach Serviceman's Pier (it also welcomed servicewomen, but not black soldiers). It featured dancing, concerts and floorshows, where popular stars of stage and screen, such as Bob Hope, Rita Hayworth and Orson Welles, came to entertain the troops. It also catered for swimming, fishing, boxing, as well as pastimes as diverse as ping-pong, piano practice and chess.

With his army buddies, Tom Cruise sampled his share of its delights about which, perhaps to spare his mother's blushes, rather than from military restrictions, he chose not to elaborate!

> I expect a three-day pass soon. I will spend it in Miami. It is a very lively place and when we fellows get together, the sky is the limit!

But there were other venues available to the servicemen for R and R all along the coast. While stationed in Jacksonville, Daytona Beach was another of Tom's retreats.

> Three of us started from camp at eight o'clock in the morning. We went to the golf course and played eighteen holes. We had a steak dinner at one of the hotels, then went to the barber shop for a haircut. In the afternoon we went to the beach and spent two hours in the water. It was swell. In the evening we took in a show at the theatre, had supper and spent a couple of hours dancing. We then returned to camp after a perfect day.

Stylish Palm Beach, summer home of the rich and famous, was another of Tom Cruise's favourite recreation centres, but one also that provided an outlet for more sober pursuits. On 5

November 1942, he wrote home from the United Services Organisation club there, one of a number scattered around the state:

> This is my day away from duty. Here I am at Palm Beach. It is a beautiful place, lovely palm trees and a wonderful beach for swimming.
>
> I am writing this letter from a Catholic USO club. It was formerly a woman's club house and the Catholic Society took it over for a recreation place for men in the service. Here you can write letters in peace, listen to the radio, read your favourite book, play numerous games and meet some charming girls.

As I reread my uncle's words, I was struck by how effortlessly he had seemed to have adapted to army life. The pictures that his words created made me think of black and white war movies, of tanned, khaki-clad American servicemen, with wide, white-toothed smiles, handsome and enthusiastic. While my uncle's life may have changed almost overnight from one of civilian independence to that of military confinement, albeit in an enviable posting, his outlook seemed to be as enthusiastic and positive as I imagined it had been in his civilian job. I began to understand why he had made such a successful start to his life in America. For me his words bespoke the attitude of an achiever, someone with ambition and self-belief, the same traits that his look from the photo on my mother's sideboard had evinced.

America, the land of opportunity, responded and encouraged such ambition and self-belief in its immigrants. My uncle had gone there in a time and from a country where such ambition was belittled and undermined. I wondered if he had stayed in the Ireland of the 1930s would that ambition have ever surfaced or would it even have had an outlet? He seemed to have brought the same qualities he displayed as a civilian with him into his military life, which for now had become his focus. From what he wrote he seemed a quietly confident, well-balanced person, with few hang-ups, someone who liked his own space, yet who could be 'one of the boys', able to enjoy himself, have a laugh, make friends.

But despite embracing the American dream and becoming a defender (in the making) of his adopted country's liberty, his letters revealed that, hidden behind his new American persona, the Irish in him still lived on. His ties to his native background, the quiet backwater of west of Ireland village life, were incongruously mixed through the dangerous and exotic stage of his American military posting.

In his letters to his parents, which he invariably signed *your faraway son, Tom*, a sense of the ties that still bound him to his family and to his home place in the old country surfaced now and then in the excitement of his life in the new world.

> Thoughts of you all are constantly in my mind ... I would give anything to see you all. I hope that the war will be over soon and I will be able to pay you a visit ...
>
> How is everybody and all the neighbours? I often think of them. In fact it was only last night that I had a dream about Tom Freely [a neighbour]. I hope he is OK. I sincerely hope that some day I will shake hands with every one of them ...
>
> I was so sorry to hear about Longin's death [a neighbour]. He sure was a swell friend ...
>
> I suppose John [his youngest brother] is a big fellow now. Does Father still play cards? I remember so well the last night we played at Tom Freely's. Tell all the cousins and neighbours I was asking for them ...
>
> It has been so long since I saw you all. I am sorry I didn't take a trip over to see you, but after the war we will all get together and I will have plenty of stories to tell.

Neither America nor being part of the great American dream had quite obliterated memories of his background and home or the sense of longing to return, if only, as he wrote, to shake hands and tell them about his great adventure.

Just over a year into his army training, Tom Cruise's dream of flying materialised. In his penultimate letter home, dated 27 January 1943, he briefly indicated that things in his squadron were hotting-up.

> Everybody here in the Squadron are very busy. We just received some new bombers and can't wait to get going.

Even from this stark statement I could detect his anticipation and excitement. The letter bore no address but the spreading-wing insignia of the United States Air Force adorned the page, indicating that it was written from one of the forty-plus military airbases by then established in Florida. At the end of the letter my uncle had written the exhortation

> As we say here in America KEEP-EM-FLYING.

And flying he was by the time he wrote his next and final letter, dated 5 March 1943. His dream had come true at last.

> I am learning radio and studying real hard. I got tired of my easy office work and next week I expect to be a qualified aerial radio operator. What a thrill it is flying over the clouds. The ground looks such a long way down, what a feeling, it sure is wonderful …

Tom Cruise had finally got his chance to fly, if not as a pilot, then in the next best way. It had been a very short training period, less than six weeks, I noted, as I calculated the time lapse between his last two letters. But displaying the same dedication and determination he had shown in his civilian life, I knew that Tom Cruise was bound to get to where he most wanted to be.

His uncle, with whom he had initially stayed in America, conveyed the news of his death to his family in Ireland by telegram. On 19 March 1943 there had been a training accident. A plane had crashed while employed in a flying operation; their son Tom and the pilot had been killed. No notification as to the nature or location of the crash had been forthcoming from the military authorities.

Somewhere in the clear blue Florida sky, something had gone wrong – a mechanical, pilot or navigational error? Maybe the usually benign weather had turned against them? Had they crash-landed or ditched into the sea, I wondered? Where in Florida had it happened?

The final letter in the box was from his aunt in Massachusettes and it threw some light on my questions. The letter was addressed to Tom's mother and was dated one month after his death. It was a sorrowful letter from someone who had become more than just an aunt to a young man far away from home. As a young immigrant, his uncle's wife had welcomed Tom Cruise into her home. She had seen him develop and make the transition to a new lifestyle in an environment so different from the one from which he had come. She had been as proud of his achievements as if he had been her own flesh and blood.

And it had been to her house, his home away from home, that his body was brought from Florida. His aunt who had, in effect, become his surrogate mother, in death could share the pain and loss being experienced by his natural mother far away in Ireland.

> I know you must be heartbroken. We all feel terrible for him. We all loved Tom. He was a good fellow, a credit to us all. Every time I hear an aeroplane I think of him. It is unbelievable to think that he is gone. We will miss him so. May God have mercy on his soul.

Her own Irishness instinctively understood how the distance, the imposed secrecy involving the crash that had taken his life and, especially from an Irish perspective, not having a body over which to mourn, all served to compound his mother's grief faraway in Ireland.

> It must have been so hard for you to receive that news. I always thought what a terrible blow it must be to have a loved one die over here and not be able to be near them.

The war was at its height and Tom Cruise's body could not be brought home to Ireland. Instead he was buried in Massachusetts among those of his extended family who had gone before him both to America and to their Maker. But the Irish Diaspora had not forgotten how to mourn their dead and his aunt ensured that it would be done as his own mother would have wished.

> I wish you could have seen the room he was laid out in. He was buried in flowers and had about 100 Masses from the friends he knew. Three nights he was waked in the house and each day people were coming continually in until midnight.

The letter established that there had been a body for his American family to mourn, albeit 'buried in flowers', perhaps to disguise the physical effects of the accident. From a report in the local paper, which his aunt enclosed, additional information regarding the crash also came to light.

Tom Cruise's plane had come down near Boca Chica Key, ten miles north of Key West, the location of his final posting in Florida. The Florida Keys (*cayos* – meaning small islands in Spanish) are a coral-fringed chain of subtropical islands, which stretch from Miami across 180 miles of water towards Cuba, and which are linked by forty-two narrow bridges. Like a string of discarded emeralds, the keys, and the white bridges that connect them, separate the Atlantic Ocean from the Gulf of Mexico. Nearer to Cuba than to the American mainland, Key

West, the most southern town in the United States, was then, and still is, the most famous of the keys. First settled 150 years ago by pirates, salvagers and Cuban cigar-makers, Key West always seemed remote from every place else, its geographic isolation an exotic haven for the drifter and the disaffected.

In war-time, because of its strategic position, Key West's naval base at Trumbo Point (originally established to suppress piracy in the previous century) was reactivated as a major base for submarines and as a training location for American and Allied seaman. By December 1940 it also received designation as a Naval Air Station and its civilian airport became an army airfield. Because of the demand for airfields, a further military airfield was developed at nearby Boca Chica Key. Early in 1943 carrier-pilot, torpedo-bombing and night-fighter training began at the new naval air base.

It was here in January 1943 that Tom Cruise had commenced his training as an aerial radio operator and where he had eventually realised his dream to fly. And it was here on 19 March, while still a trainee, that he had met his death. He was due to receive his final certificate in aerial radio operation the week following.

His body was taken from the scene of the crash and, with a military escort from Boca Chica Air Base, was eventually flown back to Massachusetts, where he was buried with full military honours. The cause and details of the crash were not revealed, I noted, either in his aunt's correspondence or in the newspaper article.

The box also contained an illuminated citation, bearing the signature of President Franklin D. Roosevelt, which had been forwarded to his parents in Ireland some months after their son's death. It commemorated

> In grateful memory Corporal Thomas J. Cruise AS no. 11021400 who died in the service of his country ...
> He stands in the unbroken line of patriots who have dared

to die that freedom might live and grow and increase its blessings.

Freedom lives and, through it, he lives, in a way that hum-
bles the understanding of most men.

I replaced the correspondence in the box and closed the lid.
What comfort these words from the President of the United
States may have brought to his parents and family in Ireland, I
did not know. Very little, I suspected. Perhaps to them their
son had died needlessly, in a foreign country, in a war in which
their own country was not even involved. There was no mention of an accident in the citation, just that he had died in the
service of his country. My uncle may not have had the chance
to play his part in the theatre of war in Europe or in the Pacific
but that had been his ultimate intention and desire, as his aunt
had told his mother.

The last time he was home he told me that he would like very
much to be sent over there.

If Tom Cruise had ever thought about dying in the war it was
hardly while he was training in the clear blue sky above his
home base.

Alongside the box containing my uncle's letters, my glossy
holiday brochure proclaimed the same range of attractions –
superb climate, miles of sandy beaches, azure seas, palm-dot-
ted golf courses, luxurious tourist complexes – that had so
enthralled my uncle and which had made Florida such a desirable location for its more sinister military role in the 1940s. I
noted that my intended holiday there included some of the
same spots visited by him: Daytona Beach, Palm Beach and
Miami. But now I knew I had to add another location to my
itinerary, both as a place of remembrance and, hopefully, one
of further discovery.

FINDING TOM CRUISE and Other Stories

Route 1 in the United States stretches south from Miami to Key West. The highway took me on what is perhaps one of the most spectacular, if disconcerting, journeys in the world. The three-hour drive stretched unendingly before me, unbroken by even the slightest bend in the narrow lane that runs across forty-seven bridges, linked to innumerable keys, their names evocative of more distant times and cultures: Key Largo, Plantation Key, Indian Key, Conch Key, Marathon Key, Ramrod Key, Cudjoe Key. The spectacular scenery – lush green vegetation, sparkling azure seas, coral reefs – lured my attention from the high, narrow overseas highway that cut straight as an arrow through key and sea. Where there was a bridge, especially a long one (the one linking Marathon Key to Pigeon Key is almost seven miles long) with a low-level barrier on either side of the highway, the only deterrent between me and the Atlantic on one side and the Gulf of Mexico on the other, it gave me the strangest sensation that I was about to drive off into the blue waters below. The long, unwinding road that stretched into the distance, however, also built up the sense of anticipation, which grew as the white mile markers denoting the distance from my destination flew by. Route 1 felt like it was leading me to the end of a trail as it had, in 1943, led Tom Cruise towards his death.

Key West, all eight square miles of it, proved as colourful and unconventional as my brochures promised. This remote haven, now a magnet for the flotsam and jetsam of many nations, as in the 1940s it had been for servicemen, exuded an air of bohemian, laid-back eccentricity, augmented by a sense of its decadent, lawless past of piracy, wreckers and wenches. It exuded the impression that I had truly reached an outpost at the end of the world.

Through the palm-lined streets of the Old Town where once my uncle and his army buddies had stepped-out, all spick and span in their uniforms, army berets at an angle, anticipating the delights of a three-day R and R, now the T-shirt-and-shorts tourist brigades strolled alongside Cuban exiles, retro hippies, arm-entwined homosexual couples and alluring transvestites. A cacophony of accents and languages made Key West's claim to be a truly international retreat appear truly justified.

Having sampled the tourist trail, including Hemingway's house and his drinking joint, Sloppy Joe's (both the look-alike and the original), Tennessee Williams's arts centre, the Lighthouse and The Wreckers' Museum, and having celebrated the sunset with hordes of other worshippers on the pier on Mallory Square, I finally reached the main destination on my trail, the local library, set in a quiet street away from the tourist bustle.

I explained my quest to the librarian in charge. He shook his head.

'I guess you've come a long way for nothing. The accident that killed your uncle will not have made the headlines in 1943. Let me tell you why. The US Army would never allow details of a military plane crash that happened during training to be spread over the pages of the local press. America was at war, you know. Now, if your uncle's plane had been shot down by enemy fire, sure, then it would have been front-page news. Our brave boys shot down by the enemy, and all that. But by their own mistake, human or technical, that was another matter. Not good for morale, either now or then.'

He noticed my disappointment.

'But, hey, you've come a long way – let's take a look just to be sure.'

He opened a large steel press that contained rows of microfilm rolls.

'What date did you say?'

'19 March 1943.'

What the librarian said made some sense. America tended to hide its military mistakes (and continues to do so, as the furtive return of the bodies of its dead soldiers from Iraq testifies to this day). But now that I was in Key West, I was determined to leave no stone unturned.

To be certain, we checked every date in March in the local papers, before and after the nineteenth, but there was no mention of a military plane crash.

'Just as I thought,' the librarian said as he reloaded the last microfilm. 'And let me tell you something else. Your uncle's plane was not the only one to crash around here in 1943. There were dozens of such accidents, mostly involving trainees. Poor guys, they were sent up before they really knew how. They needed them trained up fast, see, to send over to Europe or to the Pacific.'

I nodded. 'My uncle was only due to qualify the week following his death.'

'Poor kid. Guess he had his own war right here in Florida.' The librarian locked the steel press. 'But can I tell you, ma'am, it makes him no less a hero in my eyes than if he had been shot down over there and we could read about it now in these papers.'

The librarian's words made me remember my uncle's citation from President Roosevelt that I had dismissed as just an empty military PR exercise. Here I was, over fifty years later, listening to an American, who had hardly been born at the time, voicing the same sentiments expressed in the citation; that my uncle was indeed a hero in his adopted land. Suddenly Tom Cruise's reason for joining up, even his death, began to make some sense.

I felt the emotion well within me as I shook hands with the librarian.

'Sorry I can't be of more help.'

'You've helped more than you know.'

'You have a nice day.'

Ten miles from Key West, I reached Boca Chica Key and pulled over to a lay-by. A signpost for the US Naval Station declared it off-limits to the public. I walked down to the water's edge and looked out over the lagoon-like Atlantic, so tame, so blue, so unlike its tempestuous grey-green obverse, three-thousand miles over there.

I closed my eyes and thought of him. Had the end come quickly or had he to endure a hideously long descent into oblivion, with every second seeming like an hour? Had his mind been bombarded with thousands of life-flashes of family, friends, of home, of all the trivial but cherished things he had written about in his letters? Maybe he had been blessed by a numbing sense of being in a vacuum, feeling, hearing, remembering nothing, ties to his human life already broken, his spirit already on its next journey. Either way I imagined that the Tom Cruise I had got to know through his letters and from that level, steady look emanating from his picture on my mother's sideboard had not panicked but had remained calm, perhaps sending out distress signals from his radio until the end. Had the plane nose-dived into the calm ocean somewhere out there or had it crashed to the ground, near where I stood, and exploded on impact? Although it hardly mattered, I hoped that it had been the former.

As I watched a great white heron stalk the water's edge, I knew what really mattered was not about finding out the cause of the accident in which my uncle had died. Because the librarian was right: here or over there, he had given his life and that's what makes a hero and makes his memory endure. What really mattered was that fifty years later I had followed him here to this strange, exotic outpost, on my own personal pilgrimage to his memory, to a place where Tom Cruise had finally, for a few short weeks, been able to realise his dream.

Now I knew I could look at his photo on my mother's sideboard and feel that, yes, I understood that

> Freedom lives and, through it, he lives, in a way that humbles the understanding of most men.

The Journey Home

S HE HAD BEEN too busy at the time to do anything about it. Tom had just got the bad news from the Co-op about the milk quota, her mother had been in hospital for tests and there was all that trouble about young Connor being bullied at school.

When, by sheer accident, she had felt the lump, just a tiny pea-like protrusion, under her breast, she had put it into line on the list of things to do when she had time. Yes, she assured herself, she would definitely see to it, just as things got back to normal and when she had time to think about herself. But the time never seemed to come until she could no longer ignore the fact that the lump had got larger and she more tired.

Now she was paying the price for her negligence as the dreaded words hung in the stillness of the surgery.

'I'm afraid it's malignant.'

Funny, she thought, even when she had chosen to ignore it, the exact moment she had first discovered the lump remained etched in her memory, as clear as spring water. Ten past eight, a Monday morning, getting dressed, rushing for a meeting with Connor's teacher. It was as if, quite independently of the rest of her, her mind had chosen to register that moment of discovery in some hidden file in her brain, tagged, she reckoned, FOR IMMEDIATE ATTENTION in bright-red capitals. Now, what lay inside that file was scurrying around unchecked inside her body. Like one of those awful computer icons on her son's old Gameboy, she thought, that gobbled everything in its path into its wide-open serrated mouth.

'If I had come in sooner, would it …'

Her voice trailed off in dread of what she might be told. That it was her own fault. No one to blame but herself. A so-called intelligent woman, in this day and age, with TV and radio blaring out the mantra of self-examination and early detection, had chosen the ostrich way.

'Well, early detection is, of course, always preferable in the case of every cancer,' the calm voice of the consultant reiterated. 'But in your particular case, the cancer is quite …' he chose his words with care, as he had been trained, 'vigorous.'

She nodded numbly, unable to speak and without the medical knowledge to comment upon something that was outside her expertise, yet which was now as much a part of her as her skin or the colour of her eyes. Something over which she had no control yet which had her fast-caught in its constricting grip.

'It may, I'm afraid, have already spread. We will need to do a mastectomy, maybe remove some lymph nodes, just to be sure, and then see from there.' The consultant frowned slightly as he glanced at the notes in front of him before smiling brightly at her. 'We must be optimistic. Cancer is not the life-ending disease it used to be, you know. There are new improved drugs being developed daily. After your operation, we will start you on a course of chemotherapy.'

She was driving along the Naas motorway before she even realised. She had no recollection of leaving the clinic or of walking to where she had parked the car a street away, let alone driving the twenty miles from Dublin. She looked at the speedometer. At least she had not been speeding. They were everywhere now, the Guards, with their radar guns and speed cameras. Tom said that they must sleep under the bushes along the motorway.

'Tom.'

His name spilled out into the silence.

What was she to tell him?

If there had not been a good time to get herself checked

out, then things had not improved much since. The reduction in the farm's milk quota had made their income fall to a barely tolerable level. There was no money now for the small luxuries that in the past had made the difference between living and merely existing. A holiday, even a night out, was now beyond their reach, as they struggled to cope with the essentials. Tom seemed to have aged overnight. And now this ... added trouble and expense that she was bringing home. The operation, up and down for treatment to Dublin for the next six months, with the necessity of over-nights in B&Bs and hotels.

'Chemotherapy can be somewhat debilitating, especially at the beginning,' her consultant had said. 'Better to stay near the hospital and avoid the extra strain of the journey to the country.'

And how, in God's name, would Tom cope with the farm and the children, as well as the hundreds of chores she did, without thinking, every day? Shopping, cooking, cleaning, getting the children out to school, collecting them in the evenings, the farm accounts. God, the farm accounts, the accountant was already screaming for them, she suddenly remembered. She would have to finish them before the operation and the treatment.

Treatment. It sounded more like a massage and facial at one of those exclusive spas in some luxurious country estate than a deadly dose of toxic drugs and chemicals. She really had to smile.

And then there was her mother. On her discharge from hospital, there was no question that she could go back to living on her own. Tom had been great about it.

'She'll be better off here where we can keep an eye on her. And maybe she'll be able to knock some manners into the kids. It would be nice to hear "thanks" and "please" again in the house.'

But her mother could barely walk now and her sight was almost gone. She needed more looking after than the kids.

It started to rain. The rhythmic movement of the wipers drew her gaze. She watched as the raindrops on the windscreen were systematically wiped clear away, only to reappear all over the window surface immediately.

'Your type of cancer tends to mutate, to disappear and resurface in a different guise, so we must be on our guard and adjust your treatment accordingly.'

Her treatment, the consultant informed her, would be a mixture of chemotherapy and scanning, to ensure that if the cancer decided to relocate somewhere else in her body, they would be aware of its movement at the soonest.

She thought again of the icon on her son's Gameboy. How had such a dirty, horrible monster got inside her? She had never smoked, drank sparingly and enjoyed a generally well-balanced diet. She always bought the regulation fruit and ensured there was fresh veg on the dinner table. She even cooked porridge for breakfast during the winter months, although the kids kicked against it. During May, when the weather warmed up, only then would she succumb to their pleas for Coco Pops and Rice Krispies. She had never allowed chips, burgers or chicken nuggets to become part of home fare, only as a special treat on a day out. She thought of the convenience food dished up by many of her friends, even her own sister, too busy, they said, to go to the trouble like she did. And what good had it done her? It had given her little protection from the monster that at that very moment was gnawing its way through her. She shuddered and closed her eyes.

Behind her the admonishing sound of a horn made her swerve back into lane.

She had heard, or maybe had read, somewhere that stress was now considered a contributory factor to most cancers. Maybe it was that, rather than any deficiency in her diet, that was the cause of hers.

God knows there had been enough stress of late in her life. Whoever said that country living, being a farmer's wife, was stress free should take a look through their window at two in the morning, any night of the week, as she grappled with reams of official forms, ledgers and account books that were now as much a part of farming life as milking forty cows, morning and evening, and providing for their upkeep 365 days a year. Farmers had to do the tax-inspector's, the government's, not to mention the EU's, work as well as their own. Falling into bed, feeling drained of energy, yet unable to sleep, her head too full of worries about reactors, bank overdrafts and their diminishing income. As she watched in the darkness the hands of the bed-side alarm clock edge ominously towards six o'clock, she often felt like pulling the bed covers over her head rather than have to face another day of worry and of making-do.

And now this! What had she done to deserve this added nightmare, she wondered, feeling the hot tears spill down her face. Because a nightmare it most surely was and one from which there was no waking up. This was for real, a blight, set to cloud their lives from this day onwards.

She had seen the effects of cancer on neighbours and friends and she was under no illusion as to its devastatingly invasive consequences. The routine of family life, relation-ships, even those you would have put your last cent on as being unshakeable, stretched to breaking point. Then there were the effects of the drugs on her appearance, her hair – my God, she would lose her hair.

'Every woman who has sat there before you, and indeed quite a few men,' her consultant had assured her when she had tried to apologise for her question, 'have asked the same ques-tion. And yes, of course, hair loss is as important to the patient as any other side effect you may experience over the coming months. In that regard, I can assure you, all the necessary back-up and advice will be available to you right here in the clinic, when you need it.'

Oh God, she thought, and felt her hands tremble on the steering wheel. Side effects. Her mouth was dry with fear. She was driving through Monasterevin and pulled up outside a convenience store. She needed water. She needed not to think.

The bright glow of the lights and the warmth of the shop made her reluctant to leave, to resume her journey home, reluctant to have to continue the thought process that had made her stop in the first place. As if she had absolutely nothing on her mind, she took a sip from the bottle and perused the array of magazines on the stand.

Breasts, nude and semi-nude, voluptuous and ponderous, seemed to leap out to taunt her from every cover. Mastectomy. Even when the consultant in his soothing professional voice had mentioned the dreaded word, it sounded like something that happens in a butcher's shop. To have part of her body, that part especially, cut away, mutilated. She looked at one of the specimens displayed on a magazine cover and tried to imagine what the model might look like with only one. Given the size of them she had serious doubts as to the model's ability to even hold her balance.

A crazy mirth welled within her and made her shake. She may not be as well-endowed but the effect would be the same; her body left butchered and unbalanced, a grotesque mockery of everything that made her feel good about herself: her appearance, clothes, cutting a dash in a bikini on the beach, all the mundane things in the female calendar that she had taken for granted from the time she first began to scrutinise her appearance in the mirror as a teenager, all brutally altered.

'We have made great strides in helping women overcome the physical effects of mastectomy,' the consultant had consoled her. 'From an appearance point of view, prosthesis is now much more an art form than a surgical antidote.'

All very well for him to say, but art form or no, it would still not be hers, but something false, stuck on, alien to her body. How, she did not want to know. She finished the water in a gulp.

Everywhere she looked the magazine covers seemed to

trumpet only one message. Sex and more sex. *How to Satisfy Your Partner; How to Get More Fun from Sex; Explosive Sex for Women; Five Positions to Turn Him On.*

Sex had always been good, or good enough, at least, for herself and Tom. From the start they had always felt comfortable and uninhibited with each other's bodies, which allowed them to develop in the way that suited and satisfied them both. And despite children and family worries, sex was still very much part of their lives.

'The only pleasure the bloody tax-man hasn't got his hands on yet.' She smiled as she recalled Tom's words.

How could he caress and love her maimed body? She shuddered and hurried from the shop.

In the car she sat for a moment without moving, her eyes averted from the dazzling lights of the oncoming traffic, reluctant to continue her journey, to face Tom, her mother, the kids, to answer their questions, to see her own fear reflected in their eyes. In some weird way she felt as though she was bringing home some dreadful infectious disease. And in a way, she supposed, she was. Because from the moment she told them, all of their lives would never be the same. Sooner or later they would be infected by her absences, by the dreaded side effects and by her inability to function like she used to.

Maybe she needn't tell them at all? They knew nothing about the past two weeks, about the biopsy and the fateful wait for the result. She had kept it from them, even from Tom. They did not suspect a thing. Today, she was supposed to be on a shopping trip to Dublin.

'Stay over with your sister, if you like. We'll manage. You need the break,' Tom had even said.

It was enough, she had reasoned, that she had to go through the torment that from this day would be with her every moment of every subsequent day of her life. And especially in the silence and stillness of the night, when the dread of what was happening to her, and of what was to happen, of where it could lead, would surface. All the doubts, the pain, the uncertainties, would haunt the sleepless midnight of her mind. Why inflict such suffering on them too?

She turned the key in the ignition. She knew she was being silly. There was no hiding her disease from her family, just as there was no hiding it from herself.

The headlights illuminated the tree-lined drive that led up to the farmhouse. The familiar feeling that she always experienced as she approached her home sent a comforting surge through her body. Suddenly, for the first time since she had left at day-break that morning, she began to feel a warmth creep through her whole being. It as if the fear she had carried with her on the journey to and from Dublin, a fear that had frozen her through and through, had begun to melt. The blood seemed to course through her veins with such vigour as if it had been released from some dam deep inside her. She felt renewed, confident, able to tackle what lay within her, as much as what faced her within the house.

'I can cope. I know I can and I will. I am needed and I need them.'

In any event, there was now simply no alternative, no choice to make and, she suddenly realised, that in itself was a good thing.

The door of the house flew open and her children rushed out to meet her.

'Mam, can I go on the school trip to Cork? Dad said I was to ask you.'

'What's for tea? I'm starving.'

'Gran wants you upstairs. She can't find her tablets.

Tom stood framed in the door.

'Had a good day in Dublin, love?'

She took a deep breath and followed them into the house.